HOSTEL ABYSS

Shadows in my Room

Kaushik Baruah

The characters and events portrayed in this book are fictitious. Any similarity to real persons, living or dead, is coincidental and not intended by the author.

ISBN: 9789334175271

Cover design by: Kaushik Baruah

CONTENTS

CHAPTER 1

Familiar Nightmare

It was 26th February 1992. and life in the university hostel was rough, especially in a small Remote part of India where everything seemed to be in the Middle of Nowhere. My name is Ishan, and like most of the boys I was here to study, though these days it felt like I was studying survival more than academics. The cracked walls, leaky ceilings, and the faint buzz of tube lights were constant reminders of the state of things. Everyone around me was too busy trying to make it through another semester, either by burying themselves in books or losing themselves in late night parties. We all knew this place was temporary, a stepping stone. Everyone who is sharing a hostel is supposed to possess a sense strange camaraderie, the kind forged in shared hardships and sleepless nights, but lately, I couldn't shake the feeling that I was not a part of that, as though I existed only in the fog of my own mind , unseen by everyone else.

I woke up in a haze, my mind groggy from yet another sleepless night. The fluorescent light above me flickered, casting long, disjointed shadows across the room. I blinked a few times, but my eyes refused to adjust, as if I'd been staring too long into an abyss that had swallowed the last remnants of my energy. I picked up a small hand mirror from the nearby table and saw my reflection in it. Dark circles hung under my eyes like bruises, hollowing out my face, making me look like I hadn't slept in days. It wasn't far from the truth.

The bed beneath me creaked as I shifted my weight, the worn mattress sagging under the pressure. I lay there for a few moments, staring up at the cracked ceiling, my mind drifting within the silence. Outside, the world moved on without me—the faint sounds of students walking to the canteen, the occasional shout from some distant corner of the hostel, the rustle of leaves in the wind. But inside the room, inside my head, it felt as though time had come to a standstill, trapped in an endless loop of fatigue and despair.

I sighed and forced myself to sit up. My body protested, joints stiff and muscles aching from disuse. I glanced around the room, and the sight that met my eyes made my chest tighten. It was a disaster, as always. Empty bottles littered the floor, some toppled over, their contents long since dried into sticky patches on the floor. A pile of clothes had taken over one corner, dirty and crumpled, as if someone had discarded them in a hurry and then forgotten. The air smelled stale, a mixture of sweat and mold, tinged with something sour that I couldn't quite place.

The mess felt suffocating. My eyes scanned the chaos, searching for any corner of the room that resembled order, but there was none. I couldn't take it anymore. I knew I had to confront Raghav, my Roommate. I had known it for a long time, but every time I worked up the courage, something inside me recoiled, like old wounds reopening.

I dragged myself out of bed and shuffled to the small sink right outside the room. The tap squealed as I turned it on, the cold water splashing against my hands, numbing them for a moment. I splashed my face and looked at myself in the mirror again. It was like staring at a stranger. I wanted to brush my teeth, to shake off the feeling of filth clinging to me, but my t made it hard to focus.

"I can't keep doing this, I can't take more of this" I muttered under my breath, the words slipping out before I could stop them. It wasn't the first time I had said it, but the weight of those words seemed heavier, as if the hopelessness had sunk deeper into my bones.

I turned away and went back to my room, my mind buzzing with frustration. I could hear footsteps approaching from the hallway, and my pulse quickened. A sense of anticipation settled in my stomach as the door creaked open, and Raghav walked in.

Raghav carried himself with a casual arrogance that made my skin crawl. He was two years older than me and was my Hostel senior, and from the very first day we had shared this hostel room, Raghav had made sure I knew my place. He was a Rich kid. Spoiled. The kind of person who treated everyone around him like props in his own personal play.

He strolled into the room, wiping his mouth with the back of his hand, no doubt having just come from the canteen. Without a word, he moved to his wardrobe, rummaging through his clothes to find something to wear for class. He ignored me, as he often did, As if I were nothing more than a piece of furniture in the room—something to be used when needed and discarded otherwise.

"You should clean this place up before you head to class," Raghav said, his voice slipping through the air like a blade wrapped in silk. He didn't even bother to look at me, his eyes fixed on combing his hair as though issuing commands was second nature.

I froze mid-brush, the bristles pressed against my teeth. For a second, I could feel the automatic nod building, the familiar bowing of my will. But something inside me hesitated—maybe it was the sheer exhaustion of always caving finally hit a breaking point. I didn't care anymore.

I turned to him, the words slipping from my mouth before I could hold the words back. "No."

It wasn't loud, not much more than a whisper, but It seemed as though a crack in the surface of something long buried. His hands paused , his head tilting ever so slightly.

"What?" His voice remained steady, yet it took on a sharper edge, like a chill glimmering beneath his calm demeanour. His gaze shifting to me.

“I said, no. I can’t keep cleaning up after you and your friends every morning when you trash the place every night. I’m missing my classes because of this. Tell them to clean up before they leave, or... do it yourself.” my voice wavered as I noticed him stepping closer, the space between us closing in.

Raghav’s face twisted into that same thin, mocking smile, the kind that never reached his eyes. “Feeling rebellious today, are we? Didn’t sleep well? Or maybe you’ve finally decided to grow a spine?” His voice held a hint of amusement, like he was toying with me, knowing exactly how much control he had.

I could feel my hands shaking. The familiar urge to back down, to apologize, rose inside me like a reflex, but I swallowed it down. I kept my gaze locked on his, refusing to look away. I wasn’t going to fold this time. Not again.

Raghav stepped closer, and with each step, the room seemed to grow smaller, like the walls were closing in. His presence was suffocating, his shadow looming large over me. “Stand right there,” he said, his voice low and dangerous, the playful tone all but gone. “I think it’s time for your yearly revision.”

Before I could react, his hand shot out, fast and brutal, slamming into my stomach with enough force to knock the air from my lungs. I doubled over, gasping for breath as sharp pain radiated through my body. But there was no time to recover—he was on me again in an instant, grabbing my collar and yanking me upright. I could smell the mix of smoke and stale alcohol clinging to him.

“It’s not entirely your fault,” he hissed, his voice cold and full of venom. "Looks like you keep forgetting because I've been too easy on you," he said, tightening his grip on my collar, his eyes locking onto mine with anger. “You need to remember your place Ishan. You know I can ruin your life with one phone call. One call, Ishan. Then what? Where will you be? No scholarship, no degree, just another failure from some backwater village.”

I couldn’t find the words to respond. My breath was still ragged, my vision blurry from the blow. The room swayed around me, and all I could do was stand there.

“There you go,” he said, his voice softening just slightly, but it was no less threatening. “Maybe now you’ll remember that I own you.” He shoved me away, and I stumbled, collapsing onto the floor, clutching my stomach as waves of pain rolled through me. His shadow loomed over me for a moment longer, and I could feel his eyes on me, watching as I gasped for air.

“Clean this place up,” he added, his voice almost casual now, as if the violence had been nothing more than a passing inconvenience. He turned his back on me, walking toward the door. “And don’t make repeat this again.” The door clicked softly behind him, and I was left there, lying on the cold floor, still trying to catch my breath, the weight of his threat hanging heavy in the air.

I stayed on the floor for a long time, I didn’t move. I just lay there, staring at the cracked tiles on the floor, my mind reeling. This wasn’t the first time Raghav had hit me. It wasn’t the first time he had threatened me, humiliated me. But every time it happened, the hatred I felt for Raghav grew deeper, more consuming.

I had known Raghav since we were kids. He hadn’t always been like this—cruel, manipulative, using his wealth and status to control those around him. Something had changed inside him by the time he got to fifth grade.Even Back then he used to bully me, I had been powerless, a scrawny kid with no one to stand up for me. And somehow, as if the universe had a sick sense of humor, I ended up in the same college, in the same hostel room, with the same bully who tormented me all those years.

For a while, I had escaped Raghav when he left for higher studies, I had finally been free. But now he was back, and it was like the nightmare had started all over again.

I hated him. I hated everything about him—the way he walked, the way he talked, the way he made me feel small and insignificant. But no matter how many times I told myself I would stand up to Raghav, no matter how many times I resolved to fight back, I always ended up like this. Beaten. Broken. Lying on the floor, helpless.

Slowly, painfully, I pushed myself up. My ribs ached, and my hands shook as I picked up the scattered bottles and clothes, trying to restore some semblance of order to the room. I didn't even know why I bothered. Raghav and his friedns would be back, and the cycle would begin again. My mind was numb, the anger I had felt earlier now replaced by a dull, aching hopelessness.

I got ready for class,I threw my bag over my shoulder, its weight a familiar burden that seemed to drag me down to reality. The narrow hostel corridor stretched out before me, the faint sounds of life around me barely registering—the soft thud of doors closing, the quiet shuffling of slippers, distant voices muffled by the walls. It all felt distant, as if I was moving through a dream, my mind a thousand miles away from the world around me.

As I reached the common area and my eyes landed on the wall clock, a sinking feeling took over. I was already half an hour late for class. A sigh escaped me, my shoulders dropping under the weight of the realization. What was the point of rushing now? I'd missed too much to make any of it worthwhile.

With a sense of defeat washing over me, I turned back toward the room, tossed my bag onto the table without a second thought, and let myself fall onto the bed. The old mattress groaned under my weight as I lay there, staring blankly at the ceiling, the weight of everything—of life, of exhaustion, of disappointment—settling deeper into my chest.

CHAPTER 2

The Pouch

I realized that I must have fallen asleep the instant I hurled myself into the bed as I lay stretched on my bed, sleepy and confused. The weariness from the previous night had overtaken me and abruptly pulled me under. My body felt as though it had melted into the bed, too exhausted to move, and my bag was still sitting at the side of the bed, where I had dropped it.

I had attempted to study at one point in the hopes of using my free time till the following lesson, but it had failed. Almost as soon as I started, my focus wavered, like a frail candle fighting the wind. Now, the book I was reading was spread out on my my chest, its pages meaningless as the words blurred together. I have now missed a few more classes, not that it mattered much at this point.

It was already late afternoon, and the room was streaked with drab light from the slanted window. The debris left by yesterday night's mayhem, which I reluctantly cleaned up, was lit by the waning light. A deep ache in my gut persisted despite the passing of hours, and the sight of it all brought back the frustration.

I took a quick look around the room, taking in the familiar, unremarkable details. It was a basic space on the first floor of the hostel—two single beds, one on each side, a window on the right and another behind me, and a door at the opposite end.

Outside the window, faint voices and footsteps drifted up from the courtyard below. Raghav had claimed an extra table in the room, but it wasn't for studying. His books and papers were buried beneath clutter: old chip packets, a stray cricket magazine, a coffee mug with a cracked handle, all collecting dust as they sat untouched for weeks.

In contrast, my bed was a state of well-organized chaos. Perhaps it was habit or an unconscious need for a semblance of control, but I preferred to maintain things a certain way. Despite the occasional breeze from the windows, the room had a lingering stench that was a combination of dust and something stale.

At this point I had nothing to do, anf i did not want to study. I had to break the boredom somehow. I rolled off the bed and squatted down by the side, searching under it for something. Something familiar touched my fingers. I took it out: an old, battered cricket ball with faded, scuffed deep red leather. Years ago, my father gave me this ball, which I didn't completely appreciate at the time. However, it now had a positive nostalgia attached to it. The thought of my father makes me melancholy . I hadn't spoken to him in a while.

Sitting on my bed, I turned the cricket ball in my hands, feeling the rough texture beneath my fingertips. I stood up, restless, needing to move, to do something. I tossed the ball lightly against the wall and caught it with ease. The rhythmic thud of leather against plaster filled the silence. I tossed it again, a little harder this time, catching it on the rebound. The repetitive motion brought a strange kind of calm, the room around me fading into the background.

I'd had a lot of practice playing alone like this. when I was a kid, it was just me and that ball, a solitary game where I could lose myself for hours. The repetition had always brought a strange sense of calm, the simple act of throwing and catching created a kind of rhythm that soothed me when nothing else could.

Thud. Catch. Thud. Catch.

Until I missed.

The ball bounced off the wall at a strange angle and thumped loudly against Raghav's closet top. As I saw the stack of items Raghav had carelessly balanced there—old notebooks, a rolled-up poster, and a plastic bottle—come tumbling down, my heart missed a beat. Panic building, I hurried over and muttered a curse. There would be questions if Raghav saw this mess, and I wasn't in the mood for being questioned.

Something attracted my attention as I knelt down to collect the falling objects. A little, frayed pouch was buried in the rubble.It looked like a pouch that old Assamese women carried for convinience, that holds beetlenut or sometimes money. The dark fabric, which was wrapped firmly with a black string and had tattered edges, gave it an old world appearance. Strange symbols were scrawled across its surface, faded but still visible. Sanskrit, maybe? There was something unsettling about the pouch, something that tugged at my curiosity despite the unease creeping in.

I hesitated, my rational mind telling me to leave it alone. But the allure was stronger. My fingers itched to touch it, to see what was inside. I picked it up, the fabric rough and almost brittle under my touch. The cord was tied in a tight knot, as though whoever sealed it didn’t want it opened easily.

Before I could stop myself, my fingers were already working at the knot, fumbling slightly as the tightly wound string loosened under my touch. I hesitated for a second, feeling the weight of the pouch in my hand, a strange sense of anticipation building in the pit of my stomach. What was I doing? I should stop, but curiosity tugged at me, refusing to let go. Slowly, carefully, I undid the final twist of the knot, and with a faint rustle, the pouch's mouth opened, releasing a musty, long-forgotten scent into the air. My heart quickened as I leaned in to peer inside, expecting something ordinary—maybe a handful of coins or old keys, relics of some kind.

But then I heard footsteps.

They were soft at first, barely noticeable, but quickly grew louder, closer. My heart missed a beat, and my body grew tense. My first thought was Raghav—back early and about to discover the mess I'd made again. Panic surged through me. These weren't casual, heavy steps, but brisk and frantic, like someone charging toward the door with purpose. My hands trembled as I shoved the pouch under the wardrobe. I stood frozen, dreading what would happen if Raghav walked in.

The footsteps halted right outside the door.

"Ishan, you in there?" The voice was familiar-laid-back, almost teasing. It was Arjun, my classmate.

I exhaled the breath I hadn't realized I'd been holding and pulled open the door. Arjun was waiting in the hall, bracing his weight on the doorframe, one eyebrow arched, the half-smile twisting his lips. "Skipping class again?" His tone carried the familiar ease of someone who always managed to slip out of trouble. "No, I just need to tidy up first." I gestured vaguely toward the mess near Raghav's wardrobe, hoping my voice stayed steady. "I accidentally knocked over some of Raghav's things."

Arjun's stepped inside without asking, looking around with curiosity, he is a kind of person to overanalyze everything and often times he figures things out with simple hints.

"Raghav's gonna love that," he said, smiling, he dropped down into a crouch beside me, reaching for a few of the notebooks, and other odds and ends, to lazily flip through one as if it was some waiting room magazine at the dentist's office. "You're rather lucky he's not back yet. "I definitely don't want to be here when he notices this."

I forced a laugh. "Yeah, tell me about it."

We worked in silence for a bit, the tension in the room heavy even as Arjun kept things light. "Why are there so many books here? Does Raghav even read them? I only ever see him out partying."

"He's actually pretty good at academics," I murmured, barely paying attention. I couldn't stop glancing at the wardrobe, precisely at the spot where I'd put the pouch. That peculiar ill-easy feeling was still chomping away.

For a second, Arjun's gaze followed mine."Looks like you slept even less than usual," he said, his eyes narrowing as if he were trying to read between the lines.

"Is it that obvious?" I forced a smile, though it barely reached my face. "It's not just that, though. I feel like I'm going to be sick. Raghav hit me pretty hard in the gut this morning. It Feels like everything inside is twisted up."

Arjun sighed, leaning back , clearly conflicted. "I want to tell you to stand up for yourself, but honestly... I don't even know what I'd do if I were in your shoes," he admitted, his voice soft, unsure. "These situations, they're... complicated."

I nodded slightly, not surprised. "Yeah.. and after all these years, I am still not used to it."

Arjun rubbed the back of his neck, then continued, almost thinking out loud. "You know, bullies always go after people they believe are weaker. It's about control. They thrive off intimidation, aggression... it's their way of asserting dominance. A lot of the time, it's because they've got their own issues—low self-esteem, anger, frustration.They tend to take it out on others. It's... like, they lash out because it makes them feel less small or powerless. And if they are in a groups where that behaviour is tolerated or even rewarded, it just gets worse. They feed off the attention, the validation, even if it's fear."

I sighed, feeling the frustration well up inside me. "Arjun, man, I don't care about his reasons for being a bully. Spitting out textbook stuff doesn't help me right now." I leaned forward, clutching my stomach, the dull ache still lingering from earlier. "I'm just doing my best to get through the day, you know? Knowing he's got issues isn't going to make him stop or make it any easier for me to deal with."

Arjun's eyes softened, and he looked away for a moment, clearly feeling bad. "I'm just... I'm just trying to help" he said quietly.

"I appreciate it, but it's not about figuring out why he is the way he is. The fact is, he holds too much power over me. Over everyone, really." I looked down at the floor, feeling the weight of it all pressing down again. "I've got no way to fight back. He's got connections, money..He knows where my house it, who my friends are , everything. he could ruin everything for me with one phone call."

Arjun nodded slowly. "Yeah, but you know what? No one actually likes him, you know? People just hang around him for his money or out of fear. They laugh at his jokes, follow his lead... but behind his back, they hate him just as much as you do. They're just too afraid to speak up".

"No. Not as much as I do," I murmured quietly.

Arjun let it drop sensing the gloomy atmosphere in the room, standing up and dusting off his hands. "You've got guts at least. Most people wouldn't touch Raghav's stuff unless they had a death wish." He chuckled, but then his voice softened. "Look, just don't skip the afternoon classes after lunch, alright? You've been missing too many. Kapoor sir is breathing down everyone's neck about attendance, and your name comes up regularly "

I nodded, my mind elsewhere. "Yeah, lunch sounds good. Let's go grab a bite."

As Arjun left the room, I checked a final time to see if everything looked as they were before, I hunched back down beside the wardrobe, meaning to drag the pouch out and put it at it's original place. But when I reached underneath the wardrobe, my hand came up empty. The pouch was gone. I stiffened; my breath hitched in my throat. I was sure I had left it there just a few minutes ago.. Suddenly, my heart kicked into high gear, and I slung myself onto the dusty floor again, fingers scrambling over the surface, feeling for something, anything. Nothing. No pouch. No trace.

I got up slowly. My mind was hopping: Had Arjun seen it? Had somebody else come in? But how could that be? There had been nobody else here.

The door creaked open once more .Arjun asked with an amused glint on his face. "You coming or what?"

"Yeah, yeah, just give me a second." My voice was too even, too smooth for my racing heart. Arjun's eyes lingered on me a beat longer .

I decided there was nothing i could do for now. I locked the room and went along with Arjun, I can only hope Raghav doesn't find out about the pouch.

CHAPTER 3

Music In The Dark

The night was thick with darkness, the kind that seemed to swallow sound, making everything feel muffled and distant. I lay on my bed, staring at the ceiling, my thoughts tangled in the strange events of the day. The room was unusually quiet, offering a rare sense of solitude. Raghav didn't notice the mess I made before so that was a relief. He had gone out to some party, which meant he wouldn't be back until morning. For the first time in a while, I had the space to myself.

I rarely get the chance to be alone in the room, so when the opportunity finally presented itself, It was clear I had to make the most of it. With some much-needed quiet time, I figured it was a good moment to catch up on my studies After studying for a while, I decided to finish up some homework assignments that had been lingering on my to-do list. I remembered about the multiple classes I missed and needed to catch up on the notes. Luckily, Arjun had generously lent me his class notes, so I spent some time reviewing them and jotting down anything I missed. It felt productive to finally get organized, and I appreciated Arjun's help in making sure I didn't fall behind.

When it was time to sleep , I shifted in bed, trying to push away the thoughts about the missing pouch . Outside, the wind howled softly, rattling the old windowpanes. I pulled the blanket tighter around myself and closed my eyes. I needed sleep—but every time I tried to let my mind drift, it returned to the pouch, to the shadows that seemed to flicker in the corners of the room, to the feeling of something unseen watching me.

Just sleep, I told myself. But the thought gnawed at me, burrowing deeper into my consciousness. I rolled over and glanced at the clock beside my bed: 12 AM. The night stretched out ahead of me like an endless tunnel, the darkness pressing in on all sides.

Suddenly, I heard it.

A sound, faint but distinct, like someone running past my door. The clink of payal—ankle bells—jingling with each hurried step. It felt oddly out of place in the silent, empty corridors of the hostel at this hour.

I frowned, sitting up slightly, listening. Nothing. Just the quiet hum of the night settling back in. I shook my head. Maybe it was just my imagination, my mind playing tricks on me. I lay back down, trying to let the tension drain from my body.

But then it happened again. The same hurried footsteps, the same soft clink of payal ringing just outside my door, like someone running in circles around the hallway.

My heart started to beat faster now. I couldn't ignore it any longer. Something was wrong. But still, I tried to convince myself it was nothing. Maybe just the wind playing tricks on me.

I sat up, my heartbeat racing in my chest. I covered my ears with my hands, trying to block out the sound, trying to pretend it wasn't real. But the sound persisted, growing louder, more desperate.

With trembling hands, I reached for the light switch beside my bed and flicked it on. As soon as the light illuminated the room, the sound stopped. The silence that followed was heavy, unnerving. I sat there, staring at the now-quiet space, my heart still pounding. The sound had vanished, but the eerie stillness it left behind was almost worse.

Suddenly, the lights went out, plunging the room into complete darkness.

"Who's there?" I yelled, my voice echoing through the room.

Suddenly, the dim light above me flickered back on for a brief moment, only to shut off once more. Then, just as abruptly, the bulb started to turn on and off erratically, its glow stuttering in quick bursts. It was almost as if the room itself was breathing with the flickers, teasing me with glimpses of light before plunging everything back into darkness once again, leaving an unsettling stillness in the air.

I gasped, panic surging through me, cold and sharp. My hands fumbled for the lamp in my table, fingers shaking as I finally grasped it and light it up. The weak glow of light cast jagged shadows on the walls, and the sound was gone.

Without thinking, I scrambled out of bed and darted toward the door. My only thought was to get out of the room, to find somewhere with lights. I yanked the door open, my hand still shaking, the lamp bouncing wildly in the gloom.

And then, out of nowhere—

"Boo!"

A blinding light flashed in my eyes as a figure loomed in the doorway, holding a lamp in front of his face, casting long, exaggerated shadows over his features. I gasped and stumbled back, a heavy beat echoing in my chest.

It was Raghav.

He stood there with a smug grin plastered across his face, the torch in hand, lighting up his sharp features like a monster from a horror film. “What’s wrong, Ishan? You look like you’ve seen a ghost,” he teased, barely able to contain his laughter.

Before I could catch my breath, more figures emerged from the darkness. Raghav’s friends, one by one, appeared in the hallway, laughing and clapping each other on the back. One of them held up a small payal in his hand, shaking it mockingly.

Leaning against the doorframe, Raghav’s voice dripped with satisfaction. One of his friends flicked the main switch outside the room on and off, making the lights flicker, playing with the eerie atmosphere. The switch outside was for emergency ,with one flick, the hostel managers could cut power to the entire room, safeguarding against the forgotten appliances of absent-minded students and the potential disasters they might spark. But these guys found a use for it to play a cliché prank on me.

“Did he piss his pants?” one of them added, laughing so hard he wiped tears from his eyes.

I could feel the blood rushing to my cheeks, a mixture of embarrassment and anger flooding through me. My legs felt weak, and before I could steady myself, I slumped to the ground, the lamp in my hand falling with a soft clatter.

As the laughter reached its loudest point, the hostel’s receptionist interrupted from the corridor. "Raghav, there's a call for you."

Raghav, still grinning, shot back, "At this hour? Who’s calling?"

The receptionist’s reply was calm but carried a weight that immediately changed the mood. "It’s your father."

Raghav’s grin disappeared instantly. His face went pale, and his cocky demeanor vanished in an instant. Without saying a word, he raised his hand to silence the group. The laughter died down immediately, replaced by an awkward, heavy silence.

"Did he... did he say what he wanted?" Raghav asked, his voice sounding suddenly unsure.

"No idea," the receptionist replied, "but there's a car waiting outside, and it looks like it's from your house."

Raghav, who moments ago had been the loudest and most confident of them all, now spoke with a calm, almost subdued tone. “Yes... okay, I'm coming,” he muttered, before walking off to answer the call.

I stood there, watching him in stunned silence. The arrogant, mocking Raghav from just moments before had disappeared, replaced by someone completely different. His father must have been on the other end of the line, because the change in Raghav was undeniable—his voice, his expression, everything about him was now stripped of the bravado he had worn so easily just a short while ago.

The laughter in the room evaporated. Raghav's friends exchanged confused glances, unsure of what was happening. One by one, his friends shuffled out of the room, murmuring to each other in hushed tones. The sound of their footsteps faded into the distance, leaving me alone again.

The silence that followed was heavy, suffocating. I sat on the floor, staring at the empty space where Raghav had stood just moments before.
I picked myself up, and tried t turn on the switch again for the room. shut the door and sat back on my bed

I had no idea when Raghav would be back, so I left the door open The room was dark now, with the light switched off, and I lay on my bed, trying to fall asleep again. But no matter how hard I tried, I couldn't shake the faint jingling of payal—the anklet bells that kept ringing in my head. I squeezed my eyes shut, willing the sound to disappear. Was it just a trick of my tired mind? Or was it real? It felt unnervingly real, like someone was playing the same cruel joke all over again.

Then, out of nowhere, right behind my ear, the unmistakable

sound of the payal rang again, clear and sharp. My body reacted before I could think, and I shot out of bed in a panic, my heart pounding.

Just as I stood, startled and confused, Raghav burst into the room. He didn't speak, didn't make any of his usual snide comments. Instead, without saying a word he turned on the lights and, he went straight to his wardrobe and began packing his things. His face was pale, his expression grim, and his eyes moved frantically around the room as though everything had suddenly taken on a new meaning, a new weight.

"I have to go," he muttered under his breath, his voice tense, barely audible. He grabbed a bag from his wardrobe and started shoving clothes into it with reckless speed, as if he couldn't leave fast enough. His movements were hurried and anxious, like he was racing against time. I asked him what was going on, but Raghav didn't answer. His focus was entirely on leaving as quickly as possible.

As Raghav hurriedly packed his things, pulling clothes out of his wardrobe and tossing them into a bag, he paused for a moment and glanced around the room. His eyes scanned the floor and the furniture before he turned to me with a slightly furrowed brow.

"Hey... did you happen to find something here?" he asked, his voice sounding distracted, like his mind was somewhere else.

I felt a sudden jolt of anxiety. Was he talking about the purse? My mind immediately raced to the possibility that he knew something, but I tried to keep my expression neutral.

"Find what?" I responded cautiously, trying not to let my concern show. My heart beat a little faster as I waited for his reply, hoping he wouldn't mention anything specific.

Raghav looked at me for a second, then shook his head, brushing the question off as if it wasn't that important after all. "No, nevermind. I'll find it later," he muttered, turning his attention back to his hasty packing. His tone made it clear he wasn't in the mood to press the issue any further, but the way he'd asked left me uneasy.

Within minutes, he was gone. The door slammed behind him, leaving the room filled with an eerie silence. I stood there, stunned, still trying to process what had just happened.

The night had reclaimed the hostel, the stillness once again creeping back into the corners of the room. I turned off the light once again and crawled back into bed, pulling the blanket tight around myself.

I was utterly exhausted, my body weighed down by the events of the day and the lingering tension in the room. Despite the unsettling fear that still haunted me, the constant replay of the payal's eerie sound in my mind, I made a conscious decision to ignore it. My mind was too tired to keep worrying, and I just needed rest. I told myself it was nothing, that I'd been imagining things, and gradually, I let go of the fear.

Before long, the exhaustion overtook me completely, and I drifted off into sleep, the worries fading into the background, if only for the night.

CHAPTER 4

Welcome Visitor

It was 27th February 1992.I woke to the sound of scratching.At first, it was faint, like a distant rustling that could have easily been mistaken for the wind scraping a branch against the window. But the sound persisted, growing sharper and more insistent until it pulled me fully out of the fog of sleep. My eyes cracked open, and I took in the pale grey light filtering through the curtains. The scratching continued.

I blinked, trying to orient myself. The clock on my desk read 7:17 a.m.—too early to be fully awake, too late to slip back into sleep. But that sound at the window demanded my attention.

Swinging my legs over perched on the bed's edge, I felt the cold floor jolt me awake. The hostel room felt small, suffocating at times, but in the half-light of dawn, it seemed vast, as if the shadows had stretched overnight. I moved toward the window.

When I pulled back the curtain, I felt a strange sense of relief.

It was just the black cat.

The same stray that had visited me many times before. Its sleek, shadowy body was pressed against the window, and it pawed at the glass again, the source of the scratching that had woken me. Its greenish-yellow eyes glowed faintly in the dim light, watching me with an almost knowing intensity.

“You again,” I muttered, shaking my head. The cat had become a familiar presence over the past few weeks, always finding its way to my window. I didn’t mind. There was something comforting about its visits, like it was checking on me in some way.

I unlatched the window and slid it open. The cat slipped inside with a fluid grace, brushing against my leg before wandering toward the centre of the room.

I crouched down and grabbed the pack of biscuits I kept in my desk drawer. “You must be hungry,” I said, tossing a few onto the floor. The cat meowed softly, almost approvingly, and began to eat, its movements delicate and precise.

I sat back and watched it. There was something calming about its presence, the quiet rhythm of it soothing my nerves. I reached out to stroke its sleek fur, and it purred softly in response, its body warm under my hand. For a while, it felt like the rest of the world didn’t exist—just me and the cat, in the silence of the early morning.

After feeding the cat a few more biscuits, I stood up to get ready for the day. Splashing cold water on my face, I washed away the last remnants of sleep and tried to shake off the eerie feeling from the night before. The memory of Raghav’s sudden departure still lingered, unsettling and strange. I couldn't shake the image of him, reduced from arrogance to fear in a matter of seconds.

When I returned to the room, I expected to see the cat finishing the last of the biscuits. But instead, it was sitting completely still, staring intently at the far corner of the room. Its body was tense, ears pricked, eyes glowing unnervingly. I paused, frowning. The cat had never behaved this way before.

I followed its gaze, squinting into the gloom of the corner. Nothing was there—just some scattered shoes and a pile of papers. But the cat remained fixed on that spot, its tail flicking once before going still again.

"What is it?" I whispered, more to myself than to the cat.

I offered another biscuit, but it ignored me, its entire focus still absorbed by the shadowy corner. A nervous laugh escaped me as I stood up, trying to shake off the unease . "Okay, time for you to go," I said, bending to pick the cat up. It didn't resist, but its eyes stayed glued to that corner, even as I carried it to the window and let it out.

The cat slipped out silently, disappearing into the early morning mist. I shut the window behind it and locked the door as I headed out for the day, trying to push the weirdness of the morning aside.

* * *

After class, I finally found some time to sit at my desk and attempt to study. It was a rare moment of peace, and I felt a small sense of relief wash over me. For once in what seemed like ages, I wasn't rushing between tasks, and I could focus on my work without feeling the weight of everything else looming over me. I opened my book and began reading, the soft rustle of pages being the only sound in the quiet room. Time seemed to slip away without me noticing, and before I knew it, evening had arrived. The light outside had dimmed, and the shadows in the room grew longer. Strangely enough, I hadn't bothered to turn on the lights yet, content in the fading glow of the setting sun.

My head remained bent over my book, fully absorbed in the text. But then, as I absentmindedly glanced up from the pages, my heart skipped a beat. There, just outside the window, were two glowing eyes staring directly at me. For a split second, fear gripped me—I was startled, almost convinced that someone or something was watching me from outside the window. The eeriness of the moment made me freeze in place. It took a moment before I realized I was simply looking at my own reflection in the glass.

The angle and the dim light had played a trick on my mind, making it seem as though there was another person standing on the other side.

But then I realized—just beyond my reflection the pair of eyes didn't belong to me. The realization dawned on me slowly, and I squinted, focusing past the glass. It was not a person, but the cat I met before, sitting quietly on the other side of the window, its eyes fixed intently on me. It was almost unnerving how still it was, just staring without blinking, as though it had been watching me for a while.

With a sigh of annoyance, I asked out loud, "What do you want now?" The cat, of course, gave no response. It just sat there, unbothered by my question, its gaze unwavering. I thought for a moment that it might leave, but then, without any warning, it lunged forward and bumped its head against the glass with a loud thud. The sudden noise startled me, and I jumped in my chair.

Shaking off the lingering tension, I stood up, opened the window, and tried to shoo the cat away. It didn't move at first, remaining stubbornly in place as if it hadn't heard me at all. For a few moments, it just sat there, staring at me, or maybe beyond me with that same eerie focus. Then, as if something had suddenly clicked in its mind, it blinked, looked around like it had just woken up from a trance, and without any further fuss, it turned around and sauntered off into the growing darkness.

I stood by the window for a few seconds longer, watching it disappear into the night, feeling strangely unsettled by the whole encounter. Then, with a shrug, I turned back to my desk and flipped on the lights, determined to finish my reading—but that feeling of being watched lingered in the back of my mind.

I read for a little while longer, though my focus began to wane. Eventually, hunger got the better of me, and I decided it was time to head down for dinner. The thought of hostel food wasn't exactly appealing—I had never been a fan of the bland, repetitive meals they served—but I knew I had to eat something.

I decided, for once, to call it a night earlier than usual. There was something comforting about the idea of slipping under the covers and letting the day fade away, even though a vague sense of unease still lingered in the air. I shrugged it off, thinking a good night's sleep would shake it off, and began preparing for bed, eager to let the weight of sleep carry me off sooner than I had planned.

* * *

I woke up as I felt an icy chill in the air. The room was far colder than it should have been, and the sudden drop in temperature sent a shiver through me. I squinted, blinking a few times to clear my vision, struggling to rid myself of the sleep, wondering what could be causing this.

I hunched over, pulling my blanket tighter around me, and glanced toward the window. It was wide open, the curtains gently swaying in the breeze. A rush of confusion hit me. Had I forgotten to close it? No, I was certain I had shut it earlier, after I had chased away the cat. So who—or what—had opened it? A knot of unease formed in my stomach as I dragged myself out of bed. The cold air bit at my skin as I approached the window. I reached out and firmly closed it.

The hostel was eerily quiet, wrapped in a blanket of darkness. It was the kind of silence that only exists in the middle of the night—so profound that it feels unnatural, like the world has gone into hiding and is holding its breath. I squinted at the clock hanging on the wall: 2:13 a.m.

Sitting up in bed, I realized how dry my throat felt, as though I hadn't had water in hours. My mouth felt parched, and the thought of drinking something cool made me instinctively reach out toward the bedside table, where I'd left a glass of water before going to sleep. I fumbled for the glass in the dark, but before my hand found it, something else caught my attention.

The cat was back.

In the shadowy corner of the room, almost swallowed by the darkness, it sat there, perfectly still. At first glance, it was almost invisible—just a small, black lump, blending into the gloom. But as my eyes adjusted to the dim light, I could make out its unmistakable shape.

It sat in the same exact spot it had during the day, completely still, its body unnervingly motionless, its gaze fixed on the same corner of the room. I followed its line of sight, but the corner was just as empty as before—just a patch of darkness that shouldn't have meant anything. There is no way the cat could open the window by itself. I knew for a fact I hadn't let the cat back in since I had shooed it out earlier. How could it have gotten back inside?

I wanted to get up, to cross the room and pick up the cat, put it back outside like I'd done before. But something stopped me. I don't know if it was exhaustion, the weight of sleep still clinging to me, or maybe fear. Either way, I stayed where I was, lying stiff in my bed, pulling the blanket closer around me as if it could help me ignore my fears. I willed myself to go back to sleep, to let the unsettling scene in front of me fade into the haze of dreams.

I must have drifted off for a bit because I don't know how much time had passed when I heard it.

A soft, sickening crack.

It came from the corner of the room, the same spot the cat had been staring at, like the sound of bones breaking—sharp, deliberate, and far too close for comfort.

My body stiffened immediately. I didn't dare turn my head to look. The noise continued, a slow, methodical series of cracks that echoed in the otherwise silent room. I felt my breath catch in my throat, my chest tight with fear, and I clenched my eyes tightly, as if I could somehow block out the sound, block out the dread .

“It’s not real,” I whispered, my voice barely audible, shaky. “It’s not real. It’s not real.”

But the sound didn’t stop. The crackling grew louder, more grotesque, more sinister. I could feel it now, the presence of something in the room, something heavy, thick, oppressive. It wasn’t just in the corner anymore—it felt like it was spreading, moving, filling the room with its presence. It was there, hovering in the shadows, and I knew that something—something terrible—was watching me.

I buried my face deeper into the pillow, my body trembling uncontrollably beneath the blanket. “It’s not real,” I repeated, over and over, a desperate mantra, hoping that the words would somehow make it true, make the terror disappear. But the darkness seemed to press in closer, suffocating me, until the only thing left in the world was the sound of bones breaking, that awful, deliberate cracking.

It was all I could hear.

CHAPTER 5

Sleepover

28th February 1992.The sun's first rays slid weakly through the window, casting faint streaks of light across the floor, barely enough to pierce the room's dimness. I sat up in bed, eyes fixed on the corner I'd been staring at for hours. The same corner where the cat had been transfixed the night before. My mind was a fog of exhaustion, my muscles heavy from a night of restless thoughts, the unease clinging to me like a second skin.

With Raghav gone, I thought I might finally get some peace, but now this new trouble had caught me completely off guard.

I swung my legs off the bed, feeling the weight of sleeplessness press down on me. The room was empty now—no cat, no sound. Just silence.

Part of me wanted to dismiss everything as the product of an overactive imagination, something conjured up by lack of sleep and stress. But something lingered. Whatever had been in the darkness last night hadn't entirely left.

My gaze drifted again to that corner. It looked the same as always—just shadows and clutter. But the air felt different around it, like there was something waiting there. Something pressing against reality. I tried to ignore it, telling myself it was nothing, but I just had to investigate.

I got myself up and walked towards the corner. With a growing reluctance building in my chest as I approached. It was as if I was wading through an invisible weight, the cold clinging to my skin, making every breath feel thick. I crouched down and moved the items in the way aside.

That's when I felt something hard, brittle, and sharp against my fingertips.

I jerked back, my pulse quickening as I stared at what I'd uncovered.

Bones.

Small, brittle bones, broken into fragments. They were scattered across the floor like pieces of a forgotten puzzle, no larger than the bones of a bird or a rat. But there was no blood, no fur, nothing to indicate what kind of creature they came from—just these pale remnants lying stark against the dark floor.

For a moment, I couldn't move. My mind tried to grasp at rational explanations, but none of them held. I wanted to believe these were just the bones of some small animal—a bird, perhaps—that had somehow found its way into my room. But deep down, I knew.

I knew exactly who those bones belonged to.

* * *

Later in the day, I brought Arjun to my room, desperate for some kind of explanation. He listened as I described the cat's strange behaviour, the suffocating dread, and finally, the discovery of the bones. His face, usually so relaxed, was creased with a frown, though he kept a half-smile in place as I spoke.

"Maybe this is one of Raghav's evil schemes to prank you or something? You know how he is. I heard what he did to you a few days back” ,Arjun’s tone was casual, but I could see the unease in his eyes.

I shook my head, running a hand through my hair. “No, this wasn’t Raghav. He left before it happened. Besides, I saw the cat just yesterday. It was in here. It—”

Arjun raised an eyebrow. “How can you be sure it's the same cat, there’s tons of black cats roaming around in our hostel. Could’ve been any one of them.”

“No.” My voice was sharper now, edged with desperation. “It must have been the same one ,it came here during the day, it was staring at the corner like… like it knew something was there.”

Arjun leaned back, crossing his arms as if trying to brush off the growing discomfort. “I don’t know, man. It’s creepy, but you might be overthinking it. Still, knowing Raghav, who knows what he’s capable of?”

“What are you saying?”

Arjun shrugged. “I’m just saying… Raghav’s always had a twisted side. His dad’s a big politician, right? I always figured being that rich and powerful has messed him up. Sometimes guys like that… they do weird stuff.”

I didn’t want to think about Raghav any more than I already had. The memory of his torment over the years felt heavier now than ever, and the idea that he might be involved in something darker unsettled me even more.

I leaned forward, the isolation of the past few days gnawing at me. I needed to get away from that room, from whatever was lurking there. "Listen," I said, my voice quieter now, “I don't want to stay in this room . Can I crash at your place? Just for one night.”

Arjun sighed, rubbing the back of his neck. "I’d help, but my roommate’s a nightmare too you know. and I doubt he’ll let me bring anyone over. Sorry."

I slumped back, my mind racing. Where could I go? As a junior, I didn't have many connections in the hostel yet , nor did Arjun. Nobody would believe me if I told them what was happening. I couldn't leave the hostel, and going home wasn't an option either. I needed a plan—something, anything.

"Alright, what if you stay here instead?" I asked, desperation creeping into my voice. "You can sleep in Raghav's bed. Just for tonight."

Arjun hesitated, then chuckled. "Fine. But if I hear even a whisper of what you told me, I'm out of here."

"ok that's settled that", a sense of relief washed over me. "we should probably go bury these bones somewhere" I suggested.

We stood up and prepared ourselves to clean the corner of the room. I grabbed a broom and a bag. Piece by piece, I began picking up the bones. I knew it had to be done. There was no way I could rest peacefully knowing these remains were sitting here,

as I sifted through the pile, my heart sank further when I noticed something else— a small collar nestled among the bones. My suspicion was confirmed. It had been the cat. A wave of sadness hit me, thinking about the gentle creature, now reduced to nothing but fragments. I paused for a moment, taking in the weight of it all. That poor cat didn't deserve this ending.

With a heavy heart, I whispered a small prayer, hoping its soul would find peace. Then, I gathered the bones in the bag, trying to stay calm as I carried them outside. Finding a quiet spot, I buried them in the earth, giving the cat the proper farewell it deserved. There, beneath the soil, I hoped it could rest in peace.

* * *

That night, Arjun lay sprawled in Raghav's bed, his limbs taking up more space than necessary, while I sat propped up against my own headboard, my eyes constantly flickering between the door and that cursed corner of the room. The overhead light was on, casting a soft, almost fragile glow across the space, but the shadows in the corners seemed to resist it, clinging stubbornly to the walls like something alive, something that didn't want to be banished by the light.

"You've known Raghav since you were kids, right?" Arjun's voice broke through the uneasy silence, startling me slightly. He shifted in the bed, rolling onto his side to face me. "Did you ever notice anything weird about him? Like... hurting animals or stuff like that?"

I sighed, my gaze drifting toward the floor. "I don't know. He's always been... difficult, I guess."

"Difficult how?" Arjun pressed, his tone curious, but there was an edge to it, like he was trying to piece something together.

I hesitated for a moment before responding. "He's always had a bit of a temper, but nothing like what we've seen lately. When we were kids, we'd play cricket every day after school. He wasn't like this back then. He was just... normal. But something changed over time."

"Maybe he picked up some strange habits or was influenced by some bad company?" Arjun muttered, his tone low and sceptical, clearly not fully buying my explanation.

"Maybe," I responded softly, almost to myself. I could tell Arjun was trying to profile Raghav, probably applying what he'd learned from that psychology course he was taking. This whole situation must have been fascinating to him on some level.

Arjun shifted, lying on his back and staring up at the ceiling. "Maybe he had a traumatic childhood or something?"

I stayed silent, unsure of how to respond.

"Are we really going to sleep with the lights on, though?”

I allowed myself a faint smile, the first in what felt like days. “Not unless you want whatever’s in the room sharing the bed with you.”

Arjun chuckled, though there was a hint of nervousness in his voice. “What if it’s like... a lady ghost?” he muttered, half-joking, half-serious.

“Then we must be pretty safe with you here, they will be sure to keep away from this room” I replied, my tone teasing, hoping to lighten the mood.

“Hey, don’t hate me ’cause I’m beautiful,” he shot back, grinning.

I smiled a little.

"Hey, you know what we should do?" Arjun said, his voice carrying a hint of mischief. "You should tell a horror story."

I raised an eyebrow. "Really? Aren't you scared enough already?"

He shrugged casually, leaning back. "Nah, this is kind of thrilling. Come on, tell me a good one."

I paused, uncertain for an instant, unsure if he, or I was really up for it. "Are you sure? You might regret it later."

"Yeah, yeah, go ahead! I can handle it," Arjun replied with a grin, his excitement clear.

I paused, thinking hard. I didn’t have any scary stories at the top of my mind, but then something clicked. A memory floated back from when I was just a kid. My grandmother used to tell us this eerie tale when I used to stay with her. It seemed like the only story i could remember for the moment.

"Alright," I began slowly, leaning in to add to the suspense. "I'll tell you about the Monkeyman. It's this strange, human-sized creature that people claim roams the rooftops at night. Mostly in villages surrounded by thick jungles. They say if a child is too loud or causes a ruckus at night, the Monkeyman hears everything, lurking on top of their house. If you listen closely, you might hear it pacing on the tin roofs, waiting."

Arjun's face was still, his attention locked on me. I continued, lowering my voice to add more tension.

"Then, the next morning, when the child steps out of the house, the Monkeyman strikes. No one knows exactly when or how, but it grabs the kid by the leg, pulling them away before anyone even realizes what's happening."

Arjun broke into a chuckle. "Seriously, Ishan? That's your scary story? Sounds like something designed to keep kids quiet!"

I laughed along, shrugging. "Hey, what do you expect? I'm no professional storyteller. But it's still creepy if you think about it. It was scary when I heard it at least."

The conversation shifted after that. I told him a couple more stories. We eventually settled into a comfortable silence as the night deepened.

After a while, I noticed Arjun had grown unusually quiet. I glanced over and saw him curled up, his blanket wrapped tightly around him. I called his name, but there was no response. Turns out, somewhere between the spooky stories, he'd fallen asleep, tucked safely under his blanket.

I rolled my eyes. “Is he a child?” I said, punctuating my words with a long, drawn-out yawn. The weight of exhaustion finally hit me, sinking into my bones. Despite the tension in the air, despite the lingering unease that gnawed at the back of my mind, my body gave in. I hadn’t truly rested in days.

For the first time in what felt like forever, I slipped into a deep, heavy sleep, the kind of sleep that makes you forget everything—fear, uncertainty, and the shadows that still clung to the corners of the room.

CHAPTER 7

Scribble

I woke up slowly, my mind clouded with the kind of heavy, disorienting fog that settles in after being unconscious for too long. Sleep hadn't felt like rest; it had been more like drifting through a haze of fragmented dreams, none of which I could fully remember. I blinked sluggishly, trying to shake the weight from my eyelids, but the world around me remained unfocused and distant.

For a moment, I couldn't remember where I was. Everything felt disjointed. Then it hit me—I was in my hostel room, my own bed. The faint scent of dampness and old textbooks hung in the air, unmistakable. My senses returned slowly .

The ceiling above me was familiar, long shadows crept across the walls, cast by the evening light filtering softly through the curtains. The hostel room felt both familiar and strange at the same time, like something wasn't quite right, though I couldn't yet place what.

A dull, throbbing ache pulsed through my right leg, a warning that something had gone horribly wrong. I tried to sit up, but as soon as I moved, an excruciating, sharp pain shot through my leg, freezing me in place. My breath hitched, and a soft hiss escaped my lips as I clutched the bed. Panic surged through me, more intense than the pain itself. I struggled to process what was happening.

It wasn't just the pain that unnerved me—it was the feeling that something was missing, that I had forgotten something important. My mind raced, trying to piece together what had happened.

The last thing I remembered clearly was falling. Falling through the window. The cold night air rushing past me. The sense of helplessness as gravity pulled me down, the wind screaming in my ears. After that, everything went dark.

I glanced down at my right leg, half-hidden beneath the thin sheet. With trembling hands, I slowly pulled the sheet away, dreading what I might find. My foot was wrapped in thick white bandages, and there were faint stains of dried blood seeping through the layers. My toes wouldn't move when I tried, and the slightest attempt to bend my knee sent a fresh wave of pain shooting up my leg.

The sight of my injured leg sent a wave of shock through my body. The reality of my situation was sinking in fast—my leg was broken.

On the wooden table next to my bed, something caught my eye. Squinting through the dim light, I could make out the shapes of a small pouch and a folded piece of paper, both resting atop the table. The pouch immediately sent a shiver down my spine; I recognized it. It was the same tattered pouch I'd found a few days ago. But it was the letter that drew my attention now. My name was scribbled on the front in hurried handwriting, and I instantly recognized it as Arjun's.

I reached for the letter, unfolding the paper carefully. The spidery, slanted handwriting was unmistakably Arjun's.

* * *

Ishan,

I'm writing this just in case you wake up when I'm not around. I didn't want you to panic, so here's what's going on:

You took a pretty bad fall. Your right leg—yeah, it's broken. The university's health centre doc came by and patched you up the best he could. You also hit your head pretty hard on the way down, so you've been out cold for a couple of days now.

I wasn't in the room when it happened. I had gone to the bathroom. But I heard this awful scream coming from our room. By the time I got back, you had already fallen through the window.

Don't freak out. I've been checking on you every morning, and the doc said you should wake up soon, so I wasn't too worried. I left a crutch by the bed—you'll need it to get around for a while. There's some food on the table if you're hungry.

Take it easy, though. Don't try to move too much yet.

—Arjun

* * *

I stared at the letter, my mind racing as I tried to process everything. My leg was broken. I had hit my head. I had been unconscious for a long time. Arjun had heard me screaming.

Screaming?

I shut my eyes firmly, trying to remember the night. The memories came back in fragmented pieces, flickering in and out of focus like a broken film reel. I remembered falling, the rush of cold air, the ground rushing up to meet me. But everything after that was a blur, a blank void that I couldn't quite fill in.

But as I strained to remember, another image surfaced from the darkness of my mind. A face. No—a smile. A grotesque, monstrous grin stretched too wide for any face. The memory of it sent a fresh wave of terror through me, and instinctively, my hand flew to my own face, as if to make sure the grin hadn't left a scar.

The memory felt sharp, too vivid to be a dream. My heart raced as the image lingered in my mind, a chilling reminder that something terrible had happened that night.

I let the letter slip from my fingers, and it fluttered to the floor. As I bent down to pick it up again, I noticed something I hadn't seen before. The back of the letter was covered in frantic, disjointed words, scribbled in what looked like a rush:

pouch. streetlights. ball. fire. Father.

I stared at the words, they didn't make sense. Not immediately, anyway. But the randomness of it only confused me. There was something familiar about these words, something that tugged at the edges of my memory.

I glanced over at the small, tattered pouch on the table I couldn't find the pouch a few days ago, so why is it here, did Arjun find it and put it here ? The more I look at it, the strange symbols on its surface unsettled me.

Now, I had the impression that the pouch was connected to something. To the fall. To the strange scribbled words. To that terrible grin.

I shook my head, trying to push the thoughts away. There was a container of food on the table, and I hadn't realized how hungry I was until I saw it. Mechanically, I opened the container and began eating. The food tasted ten time better than it would normally.

As I ate, a dull ache began to spread across my head, the pain from my fall returning. The more I thought about the note, the more my head throbbed, as if my mind were protesting the attempt to dig deeper into memories I wasn't ready to face.

The room suddenly felt too quiet, too still. I needed to move. I needed to do something—anything—to shake off the sense of dread creeping up my spine.

I moved my legs balanced on the very edge of the mattress, wincing as a fresh wave of pain shot through my injured leg. The crutch leaned against the wall, just where Arjun had left it. Gripping the edge of the bed, I reached for the crutch and slowly pushed myself upright.

The pain was immediate and sharp, but I forced myself to keep going. Step by step, I hobbled across the room, using the crutch to support my weight. Every step felt like a struggle, and my body protested with each movement. But I needed to move. I needed to prove to myself that I could.

But after just a few steps, my body gave out. My leg buckled under me, and I had to catch myself against the wall to keep from collapsing. My breath came in short, shallow gasps, and dark spots danced at the edges of my vision.

I couldn't go any farther. Not tonight.

Defeated, I hobbled back to the bed, each movement more painful than the last. When I finally sank onto the mattress, a wave of exhaustion washed over me. The pain in my leg pulsed in time with my heartbeat, and my entire body trembled from the effort of moving.

I started to reflect on the last time I experienced pain like this. I think it was when I was around 10 years old. The memory feels distant, but it was during Autumn. I remember I went to play cricket . But who was with me? Was it just me, or were others there too? Maybe it was Raghav, but honestly, I can't say for sure. The details are blurry but I remember that I had and accident and broke my leg

I vaguely recall going inside a storage shed, and I saw someone looking at me from the inside. I can't seem to remember more details.

but what happened next? The memories seem to vanish after that point. The one thing I do remember clearly is that I couldn't go out to play for an entire month afterward. Oddly enough, I don't even remember the moment when I actually got hurt, just the aftermath of being sidelined.

During that month, however, something special came out of it. I got to spend a lot more time with my father. He would carry me on his shoulders and take me to see the mela, the fair that always brought excitement, and i got to eat lots of sweets. Those moments stand out—my father making sure I didn’t miss out on the joy of the festival despite my condition.

Memory is such a funny thing. I remember so many things about that summer clearly, yet the one thing I can’t recall is how I got hurt. What I do remember is the Rakh—a religious play that the villagers organized. People dressed up and re-enacted stories from the life of Sri Krishna, with dialogues and show of might between different characters. The fights were more like intricate dances. I remember being especially frightened by 'Putona', a female demon sent to kill Sri Krishna .The music in the background was chilling, and it made the whole thing feel even more intense.

I also remember seeing Raghav sitting with his father. His father's large white mustache made him stand out, and I watched as people greeted him with a lot of respect. Even at that young age, I knew he was someone important in the village. Looking back, I realize he might have been one of the key figures who funded the whole event.

After what felt like hours of overthinking, my head throbbed painfully, as if it could no longer bear the strain of the thoughts swirling inside. I turned my attention back to the note resting in front of me, my eyes scanning the unfamiliar, cryptic words once more. They seemed to mock me, as though daring me to unlock their meaning, and yet every attempt to do so left me more confused and frustrated. The strange, almost sinister script felt like it held some dark secret just beyond my grasp.

Finally, when exhaustion became too overwhelming to resist, I let out a long sigh and lay back down, sinking into the bed. My eyelids grew heavy, and before I knew it, they drifted shut. But instead of finding the comforting escape of sleep that I so desperately needed, I was dragged into a restless, uneasy slumber.

The memory of that monstrous grin lingered on the edge of my thoughts.

CHAPTER 6

Silhouette

I'm running.Everything around me is dark, the forest stretching endlessly in every direction. The only light comes from the full moon, casting an eerie glow over the twisted trees. I'm not sure why I'm running, but I can feel the urgency deep in my chest. My feet pound against the earth, the air thick and heavy, making it hard to breathe. The trees seem to close in on me, their branches reaching out like claws.

Something feels wrong.

I glance up, and there it is—something moving in the treetops, leaping from branch to branch. At first, I think it's a monkey, but it's too big. Way too big. My heart starts racing even faster as I realize it's following me, keeping pace effortlessly. I can barely make out its shape in the moonlight, but I know it's not natural.

I push myself to run harder, faster, the sense of dread creeping in. Up ahead, I spot a flicker of light—fire! It looks small, far away, but it gives me hope. I focus on it, desperate to reach it. If I can just get there, maybe I'll be safe. But no matter how fast I run, the fire stays distant, like it's pulling away from me. It's as if the forest itself doesn't want me to reach it.

Behind me, the sound of something jumping through the trees is getting louder. Closer. It's almost on me.

And then—suddenly, it's in front of me.

I stop, breathless, and stare. It's not human, but it stands like one. Its entire body is painted white, glowing under the moonlight, muscles rippling beneath the paint. But the face... I can't take my eyes off the face. It's wearing a mask—no, it's a monkey's face. Its eyes are dark holes, soulless, staring back at me.

My mind flashes back to my childhood. My grandmother used to tell me stories about this. The Monkeyman. The creature that prowled in the night, waiting for its next victim. But it was just a story... wasn't it?

Before I can think, my legs take over. I turn and run, my chest tight with terror. The forest is closing in, the trees blurring as I sprint. I don't know where I'm going, but I need to escape. In the distance, I see a small building—an old storehouse with a tin roof. I don't stop to think. I dart inside, slamming the door behind me.

For a moment, everything is quiet. My breath is loud in the silence, my heart pounding so hard I can feel it in my ears. Then, I hear it.

A creak. A low groan of metal.

It is on the roof.

The sound grows louder, the tin roof bending under its weight. It moves, slowly at first, then faster, jumping across the roof. Each thud is louder than the last, like distant thunder crashing over and over. My pulse quickens as the ceiling shakes, threatening to give way.

It's right above me.

* * *

I wake up from my dream with a startle, my pulse hammering in my chest as the sharp crack of thunder split the night apart. For a brief moment, everything felt suspended—my thoughts were heavy and tangled, still caught in the lingering grip of sleep. The relentless sound of rain pounded against the windows, thick sheets of water turning the world outside into a blur of shadows and shifting movement. It was like the storm itself was alive, swirling and roaring, a chaotic force just outside the fragile glass.

The room was pitch-dark, save for the occasional flicker of lightning that illuminated the walls in brief, eerie flashes. I blinked rapidly, trying to adjust my eyes to the oppressive darkness. Instinctively, I reached for the light switch beside my bed and flipped it.

Nothing.

Power outage. Of course.

I fumbled around on the bedside table, my fingers cold and clumsy until they finally wrapped around to find the lamp. I lighted it up and a soft light illuminate the darkness. The silence in the room was suffocating.

"Arjun?" I called out, my voice cracking the silence, as I turned my head toward the bed next to mine where Arjun had fallen asleep hours ago. But there was no reply. The room was still, save for the distant roar of the storm outside. I called out again, louder this time.

Nothing.

A cold sense of unease crept into my chest. Frowning, I directed the torchlight toward Raghav's bed. The sheets were crumpled, but Arjun wasn't there.

I swept the lamp around the room, its flickering glow brushing over the familiar clutter of our hostel space—my books scattered on the floor, an old jacket slung carelessly over a chair. But then, the light swept past something that made my breath catch in my throat.

In a sudden flash of lightning, I saw it—something hunched in the corner of the room, the same spot where the stray cat had been staring a few days ago. The image burned itself into my brain in that brief, searing moment of illumination.

My heart raced, thudding in my ears as I directed the light toward the corner, my hand trembling. At first, I thought it was Arjun, crouched with his back to me, maybe playing some twisted prank. But something was horribly wrong. The figure was too still, too contorted, and far too broad.

"Arjun?" My voice barely rose above a whisper, swallowed by the relentless sound of rain battering against the windows.

The figure didn't move.

A wave of terror crawled down my spine, and I swallowed hard, swinging my legs out of bed. My bare feet met the cold, damp floor, the icy sensation shocking me further awake. The air in the room felt thick, oppressive, like it was closing in on me. I forced myself to stand, lamp held shakily in front of me, and took a hesitant step toward the figure.

"Arjun?" I called again, my voice trembling now. But the closer I got, the more wrong it seemed.

It wasn't Arjun.

My breath caught in my throat, and I stopped in my tracks as realization dawned. The figure's back was impossibly wide—broad, muscular, grotesque. The skin—if it could even be called skin—was painted ...white. This seemed eerily familiar

Something even stranger happened as I took those hesitant steps forward. The closer I got, the more the figure seemed to shift —growing, expanding in a way that defied logic. It stretched unnaturally, its form warping, the darkness around it thickening like it was drawing in the shadows themselves. Its head, once a vague, undefined shape, started rising, higher and higher, as if the very room couldn't contain it. My heart thundered in my chest as I realized it was now towering over me, its head—an inky, formless void—stretching so far upward that it almost brushed against the ceiling. The air around me felt colder, heavier, and with every step, I felt the walls closing in. The room itself seemed to be shrinking under the weight of its growing presence.

Every instinct screamed at me to back away, to run, but I couldn't move. I was rooted to the spot, paralyzed with fear, my eyes locked onto the monstrous shape in front of me. My hands shook, the light of the lamp wobbling, casting jagged, distorted shadows that twisted and danced across the walls.

I stood just a few feet away when the figure finally began to move.

Slowly. Deliberately.

Its massive head tilted toward me, creaking like old wood as if even the act of movement was painful. My legs locked in place, and I struggled to breathe, my heart hammering in my chest. I felt a primal fear take over, one I couldn't explain—only that I was facing something that shouldn't exist.

The figure's arms—long, thick, and twisted in unnatural ways—were draped over its face, as if it were playing some grotesque version of hide and seek. Its body stood unnervingly still, shrouded in shadow. My heart raced, every fiber of my being urging me to turn and run, but I was frozen in place, unable to tear my eyes away from the figure before me.

And then, with a sudden, jerking motion, it shifted. Its arms slowly peeled away from its face, revealing what lay beneath.

I gasped, my breath catching painfully in my throat.

What I saw was not a human face. It was a mask—no, the mask. The same one I had seen before, in my dream. The same grotesque face of a monkey, with empty, hollow eyes that seemed to stare right into me. But as I continued to look, the mask itself began to warp. The mouth, once motionless, twisted into an eerie grin, stretching wider and wider in a way that no face should ever move.

Its gaze never left mine, and as the grin grew, its body, which had been facing away, started to rotate towards me. Slowly, unnaturally, the entire figure twisted. Every movement was deliberate, methodical, like it was savoring the fear it knew I was feeling. My skin prickled, and I could hear my heartbeat pounding in my ears.

Then, fully facing me, the figure began to move. Its massive body leaned forward, shifting its weight, and started to come toward me—each step slow and deliberate, as if it had all the time in the world.

Panic surged through me, but my legs refused to move. All I could do was watch in horror as it drew closer, that horrible grin never leaving its face.

Terror washed over me, cold and unforgiving. My mind screamed at me to run, but my body wouldn't listen. My legs felt like they were glued to the floor, as if I had been frozen in place. The creature continued to grow, its body expanding and twisting, its grinning face looming impossibly close.

The torch in my hand flickered wildly, casting an erratic blanket of gloom across the room. In the brief flashes of light, I saw the creature's long, spindly fingers reach out toward me, extending like claws.

Panic surged through me, and I stumbled back, my foot catching on something on the floor. I barely registered what it was—my old cricket ball, the one I forgot to pick up—but it was enough to send me tumbling. I lost my balance and crashed against the window behind me. Before I could stop myself, I felt my body tipping backward, out of the window.

My arms flailed wildly, grasping at nothing but cold, empty air as I fell. My mouth opened in a shout, my voice rising in sheer panic.

"Arjun!"

The rain lashed against my face as I plummeted, the ground rushing up to meet me. The wind roared in my ears, and in the distance, I could hear the faint, distorted laughter of something inhuman.

I head the sound of the door to my room burst open, and Arjun rushed in. His voice broke through the storm as he called my name, but the sound was distant, muffled by the rain and wind. His gaze shot toward the window, just as I hit the ground.

“Ishan!” he screamed, his voice hoarse, filled with panic.

I lay there, drenched and still, the cold rain soaking through my clothes as I stared up at the sky. My vision blurred, the world fading to black.

CHAPTER 8

At the Door

A loud, insistent knock pulled me abruptly from the depths of sleep. My heart jumped, thudding painfully in my chest as I lay there, frozen, trying to convince myself that the sound had been part of some lingering dream. But then it came again—sharp and deliberate, the kind of knock that demands attention. It was real, too real to ignore.

The room was drenched in darkness, the oppressive kind that makes every shadow seem alive. I couldn't tell what time it was, but judging by the eerie silence outside, it had to be the middle of the night. My mind, still foggy from sleep, scrambled to make sense of what was happening. I turned toward the door, squinting at its faint outline in the gloom. The knock didn't belong in the quiet of the night.

"Arjun?" I called out, my voice sounding small and hoarse, cracking slightly from disuse. "Is that you? The door isn't locked, why are you knocking?"

No reply. Just silence. The kind of silence that presses in on you, like the room itself is holding its breath.

I forced myself to sit up, my body heavy and sluggish. My hand fumbled for the light switch next to my bed, and with a soft click, the room was flooded with a dim glow. The sudden brightness was harsh, and for a moment, I blinked against the light, letting my eyes adjust. The shadows around the room bent and stretched in strange ways, casting long, distorted figures along the walls. I looked toward the door again and confirmed it was indeed unlocked.

I grabbed my crutch, the dull ache in my injured leg flaring up again as I moved my legs over the bed. The pain was there, a constant reminder of my fall, but something about the situation made it secondary. I needed to check the door. I needed to know who—or what—had knocked.

Each step I took sent a sharp throb of pain through my leg, but the urgency of the situation pushed it to the back of my mind. I hobbled toward the door, my breath catching in my throat as I reached it. I paused, staring out into the corridor beyond.

The hallway stretched out before me, empty and unnervingly still. Only the faint hum of the night seemed to echo in the distance. I glanced left, then right, squinting into the dimness, searching for any sign of movement.

Nothing.

For the first time that night, I felt truly vulnerable. There was something about the darkness of the corridor that unsettled me deeply, as though it was watching me, waiting for me to turn my back. I shook off the feeling, telling myself I was being ridiculous. There was no one there. No reason to be scared.

I reached out and pulled the door closed, the latch clicking shut with a soft sound. I exhaled, a breath I hadn't realized I'd been holding escaping my lips. I turned and limped back to my bed, making an effort to dispel the lingering unease. Maybe I'd imagined the whole thing. Maybe it had all been a half-dream, a trick of my tired mind.

I switched off the light and settled back under the covers,

the familiar warmth of the blankets pulling me down into the comfort of sleep. But just as I closed my eyes, I saw a faint glow from behind the door. At first, I thought it was just the light from a light in the corridor, seeping in through the cracks. But the glow was orange in colour , sharper, casting long shadows across the floor.

And then I saw a shadow. Two patches of shadow that looked like legs. Standing still, right behind the door.

My hand shot out to the light switch, flicking it on. The room was instantly bathed in light again, but the glow from behind the door vanished. The shadow was gone. The room fell back into an oppressive silence, as though nothing had happened.

Curiosity—drove me to turn the light off again. The moment the room plunged into darkness, the glow returned. And with it, the shadow. The legs were back, standing just behind the door, as still as before.

I stared at the door, my mind spinning. What the hell Is going on? Who was outside? And why did they disappear every time the light came on?

Then, from the other side of the door, came a knock. Louder this time. More urgent.

I held my breath, frozen in place. I didn't know what to do. Part of me wanted to turn on the light again. But another part of me, told me to listen.

And then a voice came from opposite the door.

"You should come with me"

The words sent a jolt of terror through me. My blood ran cold. The voice was familiar, but warped. I couldn't figure out where I've heard this voice

"Who are you? why should I listen to you" I managed to croak out, my voice trembling.

“I have something you want” the voice replied, with an eerie calmness. “It's important to you”

"And what is that?", I asked.

"Answers"

I felt a strange pull toward the door, as though the voice was drawing me in. That voice felt important, more important than anything else, though I couldn’t explain why. It was like a missing piece of something much larger, something I didn’t yet understand.

With trembling hands, I grabbed the small oil lamp from the table beside my bed. Holding it tightly, I limped toward the door, my crutch clicking softly against the floor. The glow behind the door pulsed, growing brighter as I approached.

Before I reached for the door handle, I hesitated and crouched down, pressing my eye to the small keyhole. Curiosity tugged at me, but I wasn’t sure what I might find. As I peered through the narrow opening, something unusual caught my eye. At first, it was hard to make sense of what I was seeing—soft feathers, dark and delicate, like the downy chest of a bird. They seemed to flutter slightly, almost as if they were drawing in around themselves, protecting something.

I shifted my gaze upward through the limited view, and then I saw Flames—bright, flickering flames—licked the air above the feathers, casting a fiery glow. Startled, I instinctively jerked back from the door, my heart pounding in my chest.

A calm voice came from behind the door. "Don’t be afraid," it said, steady and reassuring, as though it had sensed my sudden panic.

I didn’t respond, unsure of what to say, my mind still reeling from the strange sight.

"You only fear what you don't understand" the figure continued, speaking with quiet certainty. "The things you fear are inside that room of yours. You will find proper understanding only If you dare to come out."

The voice was soothing, but its words carried weight. There was a mystery here, and though I couldn't yet fully grasp it, something about that presence beyond the door beckoned me to proceed.

I stopped, unsure of my next move, my hand hovering over the doorknob. My heart raced, but that strange compulsion, that overwhelming need to know, pushed me forward. I turned the knob and pulled the door open.

The corridor was empty. The glow was gone. Darkness stretched out before me, an inky blackness that swallowed everything beyond a few feet. I stepped out cautiously, my oil lamp casting a faint circle of light around me. The door behind me slammed shut .

Panic surged through me. I spun around, but the door was sealed tight. I was alone in the darkness now.

Suddenly, a row of streetlights flickered to life ahead of me. The pale orange glow illuminated a path stretching out before me, but everything beyond the light was swallowed by shadow. The hostel hallway had transformed into something else, somewhere else. It wasn't a hallway anymore—it was more like a street, long and narrow, leading somewhere I couldn't see.

I stood frozen, staring at the lights. And then, in the distance, I saw movement. Shadows. Figures slipping in and out of the darkness. They were too far away to make out clearly, but the sight of them made me move faster.

Instinctively, I knew the darkness wasn't safe. Whatever those figures were, they didn't want me to reach the light.

I glanced at my oil lamp, its flame flickering weakly. It wouldn't last long. I had to move. fast.

Hobbling forward, I stepped under the next streetlight. As soon as I crossed into its circle of light, the one behind me flickered and went out. There was no going back.

I pushed on, the streetlights buzzed faintly above me, their glow offering some semblance of safety. But just as I began to feel a flicker of hope, the light ahead of me started to flicker.

My lamp flickered too, its flame growing dimmer by the second. Desperation clawed at me. I was too far from the next streetlight, and if my lamp went out before I got there, I would be trapped in the darkness. With them.

I forced myself to move faster, dragging my injured leg behind me. But fear drove me forward. I reached the next pool of light just as my lamp gave out, collapsing under the streetlight, gasping for breath.

I stayed there for a moment, catching my breath. The streetlight buzzed faintly above me, its warmth offering little comfort. I glanced at my lamp, hoping it might somehow reignite. To my surprise, after a few moments, the flame flickered back to life. But I couldn't stay there. I had to keep moving.

The figures in the darkness were still there, watching, waiting. And as I hobbled forward, they seemed to move with me, always just out of reach but never far enough away.

I had moved so quickly that the last streetlight flickered far behind me, its faint glow barely reaching where I now stood. The air felt different here, heavier, as if the darkness itself had substance. I stopped to catch my breath, the silence pressing in from all sides. Something drew my attention back toward the shadowy fog that lingered just outside the dim light.

Out of sheer curiosity, I turned to the left and gazed into the obscurity. At first, there was nothing but my own shadow, stretched and distorted in the mist. It shifted slightly, its form uncertain, blending into the fog as if it were a part of it. But as I focused on it, something strange happened—the shadow seemed to come alive.

Suddenly, eyes began to appear. Not one or two, but many. Dozens of them materialized within my shadow, reflecting the faintest glimmers of light, watching me. They blinked into existence, slowly at first, and then all at once—fixed, unblinking, from the fog. The sight sent a jolt of shock through my entire body, a sensation too foreign to fully comprehend.

"Keep moving. Haven't you heard the phrase, 'stare too long into the abyss, and the abyss stares back'?" A familiar voice echoed from the shadows, clear yet unsettling.

For a moment, I was startled. Then instinct kicked in, I turned and began to walk again, even faster this time.

As time passed, I noticed that the streetlights behind were flickering out more rapidly. One by one, they vanished into darkness, like falling dominoes. The steady pace I had maintained was no longer enough—I had to quicken my steps. I walked faster, the sound of my footsteps echoing in the silence. Soon, it felt as though the darkness was chasing me, urging me to move faster, and before I knew it, I was almost sprinting.

At some point in the rush, something incredible dawned on me—I had tossed aside my crutch, the one I had relied on for so long. Yet, I hadn't stumbled or faltered. My legs, which I thought were weak, were carrying me with a new strength. I wasn't just walking; I was running

The realization hit me, but I didn't stop. I couldn't. I kept running, faster and faster.Finally, after what felt like hours, I saw something ahead. A gate. Behind it, a house loomed, bathed in the same eerie orange glow from a streetlamp beside it. The gate creaked slightly in the wind, and a strange sense of familiarity washed.

CHAPTER 9

Façade

I stood motionless beneath the flickering streetlamp, its dim orange glow sputtering like a candle about to go out. The darkness pressed in from all sides, thick and suffocating, almost as if it were alive. My breathing came in shallow, uneven gasps as I tried to calm my racing heart. Then, something shifted just beyond the reach of the light.

There, where the weak glow met the shadows, a figure stood on top of a tree near the gate of the house.

At first, it was hard to see clearly. The shape seemed to waver, shifting like smoke or a mirage, but the outline was unmistakably that of a bird. Its body was covered in black feathers made of shadow, like that of an owl.. Its face was even more unsettling—two glowing red orbs where its eyes should have been, burning like embers. The figure spoke, its voice a hoarse whisper that seemed to reverberate from all directions at once.

"Do you know where you are?"

That voice... It tugged at something deep in my mind. It was familiar, but distorted, as if pulled apart and twisted beyond recognition. It was the same voice I had heard before—behind that door. Fear clawed at my insides, but there was also something else, something pulling me toward the figure.

Oddly enough, despite all the walking I'd done, the pain in my leg was gone.

"This has to be a dream," I muttered, more to myself than to the figure. "You can't be real."

"How do you distinguish a dream from reality?" the voice rasped, its words laced with an eerie echo. "After all, everything you experience becomes a memory, and dreams are nothing but memories that linger."

"You're saying this place is a memory?" I asked, my voice trembling with uncertainty. "But I don't remember ever being here."

The figure before me, a strange bird-like creature, cocked its head to one side. "Give me your eyes," it said in a voice that seemed to reverberate through my skull. "I will make you see."

Confused and alarmed, I instinctively stepped back. "My eyes? What do you mean?"

"I need to pluck them out," the creature replied without a shred of hesitation, its tone disturbingly calm. "Only then can I show you."

A wave of unease crawled through me. "What? Wait—hold on—"

Before I could finish, the bird shot toward me with terrifying speed. My body reacted on its own, barely dodging the creature's sharp talons as it sliced the air near my head. My heart pounded against my ribs as I watched it rise back into the sky, its dark wings casting shadows beneath. Then, something even stranger happened—the bird shimmered and fractured, multiplying right before my eyes. One bird became two.

A surge of panic gripped me. The pair of birds circled above and dove again, their talons outstretched, but I evaded them like before. But now, I saw that two had become four. Each missed attack seemed to fuel them, multiplying with every failed strike.

I kept twisting and dodging, my body moving on instinct as the flock grew. Four turned to eight, then eight to sixteen. The air filled with the chaotic flutter of wings, the sound of beaks snapping at me. The swarm swirled around me, their cold eyes locked on mine. Through the cacophony of wings, their voices blended into a chorus, shouting, "Stop resisting!"

My movements slowed as exhaustion set in. They multiplied too fast, their numbers becoming overwhelming. Suddenly, one bird latched onto my face, its talons digging into my skin. I struggled to pull it off, my hands trembling, but it clung on tight. With a sickening jolt, it yanked one of my eyes out, and I screamed as the creature swallowed it whole.

The pain was unlike anything I'd felt before, but there was no pause. The bird quickly moved to my other eye, and darkness consumed me. I was left blind, my mind spinning in the depths of fear and confusion.

I cried out, lost in a sea of endless black. Time seemed to stretch, the pain and fear lingering in the darkness. But then, after what felt like ages, a flicker of light pierced through the void. It was faint, distant, but it grew slowly, like a beacon trying to guide me out of the overwhelming blackness.

* * *

When I opened my eyes again, I was standing on a narrow street, much smaller than the one I had been on before. The air was lighter, fresher, and the world around me seemed unnervingly vivid. The colours were too bright, the sounds too crisp, like everything had been turned up to an unnatural intensity. I looked down at my hands. They were small—childlike. I wasn't myself. I was a child.

What is this? I thought frantically, my mind spinning as I tried to make sense of what was happening. I glanced around, taking in my surroundings. I was standing in front of a large gate, one that looked oddly familiar. Then it hit me—it was the same gate I had seen moments before, but the setting was completely different. The sun is shining bright, and everything had the warmth of a midday afternoon.

The realization that I wasn't just dreaming—this was something else entirely made me even more confused. I looked around, my small, childlike hands trembling. This isn't just a dream. It's too real. But whose memory is this?

Before I could think any further, a voice cut through my thoughts.

"Come on, quick! Throw the ball!"

I turned to see another boy standing a few feet away. He was older than me, maybe by a couple of years, and he held a cricket bat in his hands, his face twisted in impatience. My pulse quickened the instant as I realized that the ball in my hand—the same ball I had caught under the streetlamp—was now back in my grasp. My body moved on it's own , I threw the ball toward the boy.

He swung the bat with all his might, and the ball shot through the air, soaring high above the street. I followed its arc, my eyes tracking it as it disappeared over the boundary of the nearby house. The sharp sound of shattering glass echoed back, filling the air with tension.

There was a moment of stillness, a silence that seemed to stretch on forever. Then the older boy turned to me, his face pale and nervous. "Let's get out of here" he muttered, his voice shaky.

"But we have to get the ball," I said, my voice trembling with urgency. "It's important. My father gave it to me."

The ball wasn't just some toy. It was special. My father had given it to me just a few days ago, and I couldn't leave it behind. I felt an overwhelming need to retrieve it, as though leaving it would mean losing something far more important than just a ball.

The older boy shook his head quickly, stepping away from me. “No, leave it. Forget the ball.”

I stared at him in disbelief. "What do you mean? This is your house, right?" I asked, glancing toward the house where the ball had landed.

The boy looked even more uncomfortable now. He avoided my gaze, his expression tight with fear. "We better not go inside," he muttered. "I’ll get it for you later."

I frowned, confused. "But I need it now," I insisted. "It’s important. My dad—"

"No, we can’t," the boy interrupted, his voice low and urgent. "If my father finds out..."

I could see the fear etched into his face. My confusion deepened. Everyone in the neighborhood spoke highly of his father. He was a well-respected man, always praised for his generosity. Why was the boy so afraid?

Disregarding his cautions, I took a deep breath and resolutely turned away from him, determined to head toward the house. The ball was far too important to leave behind, no matter the warnings or the risks involved. My mind was set. It wasn't just a ball—it was more than that. I had to retrieve it.

As I approached the property, I quickly realized that simply walking through the front gate was not an option. Opening it would cause too much noise, and I couldn’t risk drawing attention. My eyes landed on a large tree nearby, its thick branches stretching just over the fence. Without hesitation, I made my decision. Climbing would be my only way in.

The rough bark of the tree bit into my hands as I climbed, my chest reverberating with each beat in my chest. The branches creaked under my weight, and I had to pause now and then, holding my breath, afraid they would snap. But I couldn't stop. I had to press on. The tree stood tall, and each step higher made the gate seem smaller beneath me, but I focused solely on the task. My arms ached, and my hands stung, but soon I was perched just above across the fence.

I carefully balanced myself, my muscles tense as I prepared to jump. With a deep breath, I pushed off the branch, my body lurching forward as I fell to the ground below.

The instant I hit the ground, a sharp pain shot through my ankle, twisting violently beneath me. I bit my lip hard to stifle the cry that was bubbling up in my throat. It hurt like hell, pain radiating from my foot to my entire leg. I clenched my fists, forcing myself to stay quiet, forcing myself not to cry out.

For a moment, I lay there, panting, my leg throbbing, but I knew I couldn't waste time. Ignoring the pain I limped forward, each step sending waves of agony through me, but I pushed it aside. Nothing mattered except the ball.

I approached the side yard, my eyes scanning the grass for any sign of it. The older boy hesitated for a moment before reluctantly following me. I figured the ball must have fallen near the the storage shed.

Finally, I spotted the ball near an open storeroom door. Relief washed over me as I bent down to pick it up. But as soon as my fingers closed around the ball, a strange, icy sensation shot through me, freezing me in place.

Slowly, I looked back, and there, standing over me, was the older boy's father, his big white moustache covering a sizable portion of his face . He stood in the shadow of the house, his face expressionless except for a cold, calculating smile. There was an eerie quality to it him, something dark and dangerous lurking behind his calm exterior.

"Who broke the window?" he asked, his voice soft but full of menace.

My stomach twisted into knots, fear gripping me tightly. I opened my mouth to answer, but no words came out. I glanced at the older boy beside me, expecting him to speak, but he stayed silent, his face drained of color.

The father's smile didn't waver, but his eyes turned sharp, cold as ice. He took a step closer, his presence looming over us. "Who broke the window?" he repeated, his voice even softer, more dangerous.

I felt the older boy trembling beside me, his fear palpable. Without thinking twice, the words tumbled out of my mouth. "I did. It was me."

The father's gaze shifted to me, and for a moment, time seemed to stand still. Then, without warning, he kicked his son—hard—right in the stomach. The boy crumpled to the ground, gasping in pain, clutching his side.

I stood there, frozen, horror flooding my veins. I wanted to run, to get away, but my body refused to move.

"You let this happen," the father said, his voice cold and devoid of any emotion. He stared down at his son with a look of contempt. "Did I not teach you how to keep your juniors in control?"

The boy whimpered, unable to speak, but his father wasn't finished. His eyes landed on a long, thin stick propped up against the wall. He picked it up, turning it over in his hands before shoving it into his son's grasp.

"Teach him," the father said, his voice dripping with icy disdain. "Keep him in check."

The older boy rose slowly to his feet, his expression twisted with pain and humiliation. His eyes met mine, and in that moment, I knew what was coming. His hands trembled as he gripped the stick, but there was a hardness in his eyes that hadn't been there before.

I tried to move, to run, but it was too late. The boy grabbed me on my leg that was hurt. The first blow landed hard against my back, and I cried out in pain. Tears stung my eyes as the older boy's voice cracked with rage.

"I told you not to come here!" he shouted, swinging the stick again. "I told you to stay away!
you- you shouldn't have thrown the ball here."

The blows came harder, faster. Each one sent a jolt of pain through my body, but I refused to let go of the ball.

Through the pain, I caught sight of something in the shadows beyond the storage room door. A small, dark figure watched from the shadows, its eyes gleaming with something far more dangerous than curiosity.

And then, as the darkness closed in, everything went black.

CHAPTER 10

Fractured Mind

I jolted awake, my chest heaving, drenched in sweat. My heart pounded in my ears as I lay there, disoriented and gasping for breath. The memory of what had just happened in the dream lingered like the last traces of smoke from a fire—painful and vivid, too real to shake off. It wasn't just a dream; I could sense something more. The pain, the fear—it had all been too intense, too specific. I sat up, wiping my damp forehead with the back of my hand, trying to calm my racing mind.

I noticed that my right hand felt off, I felt myself gripping something solid. Slowly, I looked down, My breath hitched.

There, in my hand, was the ball. The same ball from my dream. The one I had clung to as a child. The one my father had given me.

It wasn't just a dream. It was a memory.

The realization hit me like a punch to the gut. How could this be possible? I had forgotten about that day—the house, the other boy must have been Raghav. All of it had been buried somewhere deep in my mind, hidden for years. But now, it had resurfaced, dragged out of the shadows by some force I couldn't understand. And the ball—still in my hand—was undeniable proof that it wasn't just some figment of my imagination.

Before I could think any further, the door creaked open, and I looked up to see Arjun walking in. Relief washed over his face when he saw me sitting up in bed.

“You’re awake,” he said, a smile tugging at the corners of his lips. “Finally. I was starting to worry.”

I tried to smile back, but the unease from the dream—no, the memory—still weighed heavily on me. “Yeah, I’m awake,” I mumbled, glancing down at the ball again.

Arjun walked over and put down a plate of food on the bedside table. “I brought you something to eat. Did you eat the food I left you earlier?”

I nodded absently, not really paying attention to his question. “yes I did, Thanks...” I muttered.

"Hey, what day is it today?" I asked, still groggy and disoriented.

"It's the first of March," they replied calmly. "You've been asleep for quite a while."

How long had I been out? What had I missed? My mind raced as I tried to piece together what had happened before I drifted into such a deep, unshakeable sleep.

"I must have missed a few classes too," I muttered, turning my gaze toward Arjun with a heavy sigh.

"Don't worry about that," Arjun chimed in before I could respond. "I talked to the teachers and explained everything. If you're lucky, they might even give you an exception for the days you missed before all this."

I looked at him, a bit of relief washing over me. "You really know how to handle everything, don’t you?"

He chuckled softly. "Haha, don’t go showering me with compliments now. I just ..I like to think about every possibilities ..you know?." His casual smile masked the effort he'd clearly put in.

"Hey, do you want me to reach out to someone from your family?" Arjun asked , his concern evident.

I quickly shook my head. "No, no, I really don't want to trouble my poor mother. She'll only worry herself sick over this, and that's the last thing I want. Besides, this should heal in a month, right? ."

Arjun paused for a moment, studying me carefully. "Alright," he said finally, though there was a hint of doubt in his voice. "If you say so. But the doctor sayd not to put too much pressure on it."

Arjun sat on the edge of Raghav's bed, his expression growing serious. “Ishan, what happened that night? When you fell... I heard you scream, but by the time I got back, you were already on the ground. I don't understand what could've happened.”

I felt a knot tighten in my stomach as the memories of that night began to resurface. The dark figure, the grinning monster, the terrifying fall—it all came back in broken, jagged pieces, just like the nightmare I had woken up from.

“I... I don't remember everything clearly,” I admitted, my voice low and unsure. “But I saw something. Something... not human. It was like a monster, standing right there in my room. I backed away, and that's when I fell out of the window.”

Arjun's face hardened with concern. “I checked the room, Ishan. There was nothing there. No sign of anyone, no creature. If there really was something in your room, how could it disappear so quickly?”

I shook my head, the frustration mounting. “I don't know Arjun, but I know what I saw.”

For a long moment, Arjun just looked at me, his brow furrowed in thought. Finally, he sighed and spoke softly. “Ishan, I need to tell you something, and I want you to hear me out.” His tone was gentle, as if he was about to share something painful. “You’ve been through a lot lately, and I don’t want to scare you, but... what if this is something else? Something mental.”

I blinked, taken aback. “What do you mean?”

Arjun hesitated for a moment, clearly struggling with how to say what was on his mind. When he finally spoke, his voice was measured, almost like he was afraid of saying too much. "Schizophrenia," he began quietly. "I’ve read about it. Sometimes people see things that aren’t really there. They hear voices... things that no one else can hear." He glanced at me, searching for my reaction, then continued carefully. "It’s more common than people think. One of the main signs is hallucinations—people hearing, seeing, or even feeling things that aren't actually there. Most often, it's voices, talking to them, narrating their actions, or sometimes even telling them what to do."

“I’m not saying that’s what’s happening to you,” Arjun continued, his voice cautious. “But maybe it’s something you should think about. You’ve been under a lot of stress lately. It could be your mind playing tricks on you.”

Anger flared up inside me, my initial reaction to reject the idea completely. But doubt, like a shadow, began creeping in. Could Arjun be right? Could everything I had seen—the monster, the shadows, even the ball in my hand—be the product of a mind unravelling? Was I losing my grip on reality?

“I’m not going crazy,” I said, though my voice wavered slightly. I gripped the ball tighter, as if it could ground me. “I saw it, Arjun. I felt it.”

Arjun sighed again, standing up and resting a hand on my shoulder. “I’m just saying... keep it in mind, alright? You don’t have to go through this alone. ”

I nodded, but his words left a bitter taste in my mouth. I appreciated his concern, but the idea that this was all in my head

—that I was the problem—I did not want to accept that. As Arjun left the room, I stared down at the ball again, rolling it slowly between my fingers. My thoughts were a mess. Could it really be possible that everything I had experienced was just a figment of my imagination? Or was there something deeper at play—something buried in my past that I had forgotten?

Has anyone in your family ever dealt with something like this before?" Arjun asked, his tone probing but concerned.

I shifted uncomfortably in my seat, not wanting to delve into the topic. "Hey, come on, I really don't want to get into this," I replied, my hesitation evident.

"I get that, but sometimes these kinds of illnesses can be passed down," he persisted, not backing down. "It could be inherited, especially if you've had a tough or traumatic childhood."

I sighed, realizing he wasn't going to drop the subject easily. "Look, I'll admit it. I didn't have the perfect childhood—far from it—but as far as I can recall, there weren't any major issues in my family when I was younger. At least, not until I reached college. Raghav was the only one that ever really disturbed my peace back then."

As Arjun continued discussing the nature of mental illness, my thoughts drifted back to something peculiar I had witnessed once. It was late at night, and I had woken up to see Raghav sitting at the table, his back turned toward me. A small lamp illuminated his figure as he appeared to be studying, At first, I thought nothing of it, but then I heard him speak. He wasn't talking to me, though—it seemed like he was talking to himself. His voice was low, almost eerie, as he muttered, "I own you now, not my father. You do what I say."

At the time, I had brushed it off, thinking it was just some kind of pep talk, maybe something to motivate himself. But now, reflecting on it, I can't help but wonder if it was more than that. Given the strained relationship he had with his father, it wouldn't be surprising if Raghav had developed his own set of issues, ones he kept hidden from everyone.

I clenched the ball in my hand. I needed to know more. There were too many unanswered questions, too many fragments of my memory that didn't make sense. I couldn't just dismiss it all as madness.

* * *

That night, I lay in bed, the faint glow of the moonlight filtering weakly through the window. The room was quiet. My mind refused to settle, and even though I was exhausted, sleep came reluctantly.

And when it finally did, it brought with it a sense of dread.

I saw myself from above, as though I was someone—or something—else watching from the shadows. The room stretched out beneath me, and there I was, lying in bed, oblivious. But in the corner of the ceiling, I was moving. It slithered along the walls, dark and silent, like a predator stalking its prey.

The thing moved closer, creeping along the ceiling with terrifying grace. Inch by inch, it made its way toward the bed, toward me. I could feel its intent, the way it watched me. I wanted to scream, to warn myself, but I was trapped .

The creature's long fingers reached out, hovering just above my sleeping form. It extended one finger, brushing it against my forehead.

* * *

I jolted awake, my breath coming in ragged gasps.

There, hovering in front of my face, was a hand—dark, barely more than a shadow. I froze, my body seized by fear. My mind raced, trying to comprehend what I was seeing, but before I could react, the hand vanished, dissolving into the shadows above my head.

I stared at the empty space in front of me, my whole body shaking. Am I losing it? I thought. Was this what Arjun had warned me about? Was I seeing things that weren't real, imagining horrors that didn't exist?

Or was there something else? Something real, lurking in the darkness, watching me?

My gaze fell to the ball still clutched in my hand, the one link to my past, to the memories that had been buried for so long. If my mind was playing tricks on me, what else had it hidden? What else had I forgotten?

Deep down, I knew. Whatever was haunting me in the shadows, whatever had stirred those long-forgotten memories, it wouldn't stay hidden forever. One way or another, I was going to have to face it.

CHAPTER 11

The Bully Returns

The clock ticked past midnight, and I was still wide awake. My heart pounded in my chest, my mind racing, every nerve in my body on edge. The room was bathed in a harsh, artificial glow—every lamp and bulb switched on in a desperate attempt to keep the darkness at bay. But no matter how bright the room was, I couldn't shake the suffocating weight pressing down on me. It felt as if the darkness was alive, just beyond the reach of the light, waiting for its moment to creep in.

I couldn't forget the hand—the pale, ghostly hand that had hovered in front of my face not long ago. The memory of its cold touch still sent shivers crawling up my spine. I shifted uncomfortably in bed, trying to push the image out of my mind, but it wouldn't leave me. The thought gnawed at me, a constant reminder that something was in the room with me, lurking just beyond my sight. I needed to stay awake, to keep watch. If I let my guard down, I wasn't sure what might happen.

Suddenly, a knock echoed through the room, reverberating off the walls. I sat bolt upright, my pulse quickening. There was another knock—more insistent this time. I glanced at the clock. 12:15 AM. My throat tightened with unease. This all seemed very familiar, is the strange bird back ? Am I in a dream again?

"Who is it?" I called out, my voice cracking slightly.

"It's me, Raghav," came the reply from the other side of the door. His voice was familiar, but something about it felt off. It sounded strained, maybe even distressed, in a way I had never heard from him before. What was Raghav doing here at this hour?

I hesitated, my mind whirling. "Why are you here so late?" I asked, trying to keep my voice steady.

There was a pause, and then the voice came again, this time more irritated. "Open the door, Ishan. I need something from the room. I left something here, and I need to take it back. Just let me in."

I narrowed my eyes, suspicion gnawing at me. why would he show up in the middle of the night to retrieve it? I gripped the crutch next to my bed, my knuckles white.

"Prove me it's you," I demanded, raising my voice slightly. "I'm -- I'm not sure you're real."

A low chuckle sounded from behind the door, but there was a sharpness to it that set my nerves on edge. "Oh, for God's sake, Ishan, stop being paranoid!" the voice snapped, growing louder. "Just open the damn door! I don't have all night!"

The impatience, the mocking tone—it sounded like Raghav. But there was still something off, something I couldn't quite place. My hand hovered near the door handle, trembling, but I didn't unlock it. The knot of fear in my stomach grew tighter.

The voice outside the door shifted, growing more desperate. "Listen, Ishan, I really left something that i...i borrowed from my father. I have to bring it back tonight. I can't go home without it, just let me in. I'll be gone in a minute."

I could hear the urgency in the voice, but I have never heard Raghav so desperate before. The fear I had felt earlier surged back, stronger than before. Was my mind playing tricks on me, like

Arjun had warned? Could this all be some hallucination, a product of my own unravelling sanity?

The knocking resumed, louder and more forceful this time. The person on the other side was growing impatient.

"Open the door!" the voice barked, frustration creeping into its tone. "Or I won't let you sleep tonight!"

Suddenly, the lights in the room flickered. The room plunged into brief darkness before the lights flickered back on again. I heard a faint click from outside—the main switch being flipped on and off. The lights blinked again, the shadows in the room dancing wildly with each flicker.

"I'm not leaving until you open this door, Ishan!" the voice snarled from behind the door. "Open it, or I'll make sure you regret it!"

The lights continued to flicker. Eyes closed tight, I braced myself, clutching the crutch beside me like a lifeline.

"I'm going to break down the door, Ishan!" Raghav shouted at the top of his lungs, his voice full of frustration and urgency.

"Wait, hold on!" I called out, trying to stop him. But by the time I managed to gather myself and approach the door again, it was already too late.

With a deafening crash, the door burst open, splinters of wood flying across the room. My eyes snapped open in shock, and I saw Raghav standing in the doorway, his silhouette outlined by the dim light from the corridor behind him. But something was wrong—his expression was twisted with fury, his eyes wild and filled with a rage I had never seen before.

He stormed into the room, the door creaking on its broken hinges behind him. The lights in the room flickered one last time before going out completely, plunging us into near darkness. Only the faint glow from the corridor remained, casting long, uneven shadows across Raghav's back.

"What the hell is wrong with you, Ishan?" Raghav yelled, advancing toward me. "You think you can just ignore me like that?"

I backed up against the bed. My injured leg made it impossible to run, and Raghav was getting closer, his fists clenched, his body radiating anger.

"Do you have any idea how many times I've tried to reach this room?" Raghav's voice was filled with frustration and suspicion. "The day I left, my father told me to come back and retrieve the thing I left behind here. But every time I get close to this room, I end up waking up in the streets, completely disoriented."

"What? Why? How is that even possible?" I asked, utterly confused by what he was saying.

"Don't act clueless! This has to be your doing, right? Do you really think you can play these games with me?" His tone turned accusatory, his eyes narrowing with suspicion.

"What are you talking about?" I asked again, but Raghav wasn't interested in explanations. He wasn't ready to listen to a word I had to say, convinced that I was somehow responsible for this bizarre situation.

His rage filled the room, suffocating me as he approached. I could feel the heat of his anger, the way his eyes burned with it, and I knew there was no reasoning with him. He raised his hand, ready to strike.

And then, before I could even process what was happening, something shifted in the air.

A shadow—dark and formless—appeared from the top of the room, moving with an unnatural speed. Goosebumps rippled across my skin as I watched in horror. The shadowy figure wasn't human, wasn't anything I could explain. It was a dark, twisted hand, and it moved toward Raghav with terrifying precision.

Before he could react, the hand wrapped itself around his face.

Raghav froze. His body went rigid, his eyes wide with terror. He let out a strangled gasp, his hands flailing helplessly as the shadowy hand tightened its grip. His face contorted in pain, I saw Raghav getting lifted up in the air, and then, just as quickly as it had appeared, the hand released him and vanished into the darkness.

Raghav crumpled to the floor, gasping for air, his face pale and covered in a cold sweat. For a moment, neither of us moved. I stared at him, my heart pounding, my mind reeling. What had just happened?

Slowly, Raghav got to his feet, his movements stiff and mechanical. He didn't look at me. He didn't say a word. He simply stumbled toward the door, disappearing into the dim light of the corridor. And then he was gone.

The room fell silent once more.

I sat there, frozen in place, my entire body trembling. My mind was a whirlwind of fear and confusion, unable to process what had just happened. The door was broken, hanging from its hinges, the splinters of wood scattered across the floor. The shadowy hand, the flickering lights, Raghav's sudden change—it all replayed in my head, over and over, a relentless loop of terror.

A deep sense of dread settled over me as I realized that whatever was haunting me wasn't just in my mind—it was real.

"This... this can't be schizophrenia" I whispered to myself, my voice barely audible in the stillness of the room. My eyes darted to the broken door, the undeniable proof that something had happened. "There really is something here. Something in this room."

What was Raghav talking about? Not being able to enter the room? The more I thought about it, the more it started to make sense. I had seen strange things like this happen before, though I hadn't given them much thought at the time.

I remembered a similar peculiar incident . There was this one night when the warden got wind of a wild party happening in our room. Of course it was organized by none other than Raghav. I was relieved, hoping the warden would storm in and put an end to the chaos. But instead, something strange happened. The warden came right up to our door—and then walked past it. He ended up barging into the room across the hall, where he found another group of students drinking and causing trouble, and took took some action on those kids.

At the time, I thought it was pure luck. Maybe it was Raghav's work or, more likely, his father's influence that saved him from the warden's wrath, but this happened multiple times. But now, thinking about Raghav's words—how he couldn't enter this room no matter how hard he tried—I started to question it. ? Was there something more mysterious at work all along, something beyond Raghav's influence?

It was time for me to make a decision—do I stay in the room, or should I leave? The weight of the choice pressed on me as I started weighing what I had to gain against what I had to lose.

Whatever presence or force was in this room could have harmed me at any moment, yet it Didn't. I have stayed here for some time, and as strange and mysterious as it was, nothing has tried to hurt me. In fact, I started to consider that this presence might even be responsible for something good—somehow, it has triggered a flood of old childhood memories I thought I had lost. These memories, long forgotten, had started to come back to me.

And then there was the note. It had an undeniable pull on me, urging me to stay, especially the word "father." Could I have forgotten something important about my father? Was there a missing piece of my past that I had yet to uncover? The mention of "fire" still puzzled me as well—I had no idea what it could mean, but it felt significant.

Whatever this force is, it hasn’t hurt me so far. But how long would that last? Was it only a matter of time before something darker revealed itself? In the end, I decided that staying might be worth the risk. If I left now, I might never find out the truth. But if I stayed, there was a chance I could finally understand everything —my memories, the note, and whatever mysterious power was tied to this place.

So, I chose to remain, bracing myself for whatever might come next. Perhaps what I would learn could change everything.

Gathering my strength, I managed to turn on the light. I pushed myself back onto the bed, my injured leg throbbing with pain. I curled up tightly, pressing my back against the wall, my eyes scanning the room for any sign of movement.

I would stay awake again that night. There was no other choice. I decided to confront whatever was in here, but that didn't mean I wasn't scared.

As the hours stretched on, I sat there, trembling, my eyes wide open, waiting.

CHAPTER 12

Trail of Secrets

It is morning now. I haven't slept, not even for a moment. My eyes, heavy and bloodshot, were fixed on the splintered door. The events of the night before played over and over in my mind, like a broken record.

Every inch of me was exhausted, but sleep wasn't an option. Not after everything that had happened. My mind buzzed with fragments of memory—the pale hand, the overwhelming darkness, Raghav's rage-filled face, and the way it all ended in utter silence. I shuddered, the feeling of dread still clinging to me.

A knock on the broken door snapped me back to the present, jolting my frayed nerves.

It was Arjun.

"Ishan, what the hell happened here?" Arjun asked, stepping cautiously into the room. His face twisted into a mask of confusion and concern as he took in the damage. His eyes traced the jagged wood and splintered frame of the door, then flicked back to me, his brows furrowed.

I swallowed, my throat dry. I didn't know where to begin. "Raghav... he was here last night. He broke the door down. He was acting strange... like, not himself. It was like he—" I paused, unsure of how much I could even say without sounding insane. "I don't know."

"Did Raghav come into the room while I was unconscious?" I asked, my voice tinged with uncertainty, trying to piece together the fragments of what had happened.

"No, I haven't seen him enter the room at all," he replied, shaking his head. "But I did hear someone mention that they saw Raghav heading in this direction. They even called out to him, but he didn't respond. He looked like he was in a bad mood, angry about something."

His words left me uneasy. Was Raghav telling the truth? I wondered to myself. Could he have really tried to enter the room but never made it inside? Why, then, was he able to come into the room so easily just yesterday? Something didn't add up, and the more I thought about it, the more suspicious it seemed.

Arjun crossed his arms, skepticism darkening his features. “Are you sure it wasn’t something else? I mean, I don’t want to accuse you, but y—”

“You think I broke my own door?” I snapped, frustration rising in my chest. “You think I have the strength left to do so?”

Arjun’s expression softened, his voice gentler. “I’m not saying that, bhai. Between the fall and the… things you’ve been saying. I just need to know if you’re absolutely sure about what happened.”

My fists clenched, the tension in the room thick. I wanted to scream, to make him believe me, but there were no words to explain the madness of what had transpired. “I’m telling you the truth, Arjun. Raghav was here. He broke down the door. And then… something happened. Something I can’t explain.”

Arjun shook his head slowly, his concern deepening. “Alright, I won’t push you on this. Let’s not argue about it. I’ll get someone to fix the door tomorrow.” He set a plate of food on the small table next to my bed, his gaze softening with concern. "Eat something. You'll feel better."

I didn't respond, my focus still locked on the broken door as he turned and left the room, leaving me alone with my thoughts once again.

* * *

That night, I sat in my room, every light in the place burning brightly. The memories of the previous night clung to me like a fog, refusing to let me rest. Every creak, every shift in the air, every rustle from outside the window felt like a threat. The clock ticked away, and as midnight approached, I felt my eyelids grow heavier, fighting the weight of my exhaustion.

I forced myself to sit up, rubbing my eyes. Every part of me ached with fatigue, my eyelids heavy, and my mind sluggish, playing cruel tricks on me as I tried to stay awake. It was becoming harder to tell what was real and what wasn't. My surroundings seemed to blur but something peculiar grabbed my attention.

I squinted, trying to focus on the ceiling where a strange, thin black patch was slowly taking shape. It reminded me of rainwater collecting at a single point, but there was no rain. The patch grew denser and darker until, with a sudden plop, a drop of thick, black liquid fell onto my leg. I recoiled, instinctively jerking away from the oily substance. It wasn't water—no, it was far too viscous for that. I watched, wide-eyed, as the dark liquid pooled on the floor. More drops began to appear from other points on the ceiling, dripping in an eerie silence.

Before long, these droplets converged, forming a larger pool that seemed to snake its way across the room, almost with purpose, as if guided by some unseen force. The liquid continued to trickle, forming a thin, ominous trail that led toward the door, out of my room.

At first, I shook my head, refusing to believe it. I told myself it was just another hallucination, just my sleep-deprived brain crafting more illusions. But the more I watched, the harder it became to deny its reality. I knelt cautiously by the pool, curiosity winning over caution, and dipped my fingers into the inky substance. It clung to my skin, slick and greasy like engine oil, with an unmistakable stench.

Why was this pooling in my room? Where could it possibly be coming from? My head spun with confusion.

Just as I was lost in these unsettling thoughts, something else demanded my attention. Out of the corner of my eye, I saw movement by the window. I turned to see something even more bizarre—a massive beak, like that of an owl, pushing its way through the gap in the window frame. I froze. When had I opened the window?

The beak shifted and it spoke in a familiar, raspy voice. "You should follow that."

I blinked, trying to comprehend what was happening. “Are you the bird I met before?” I asked, my voice shaking with disbelief.

The creature tilted its head, its eyes gleaming with an ancient, knowing look. “You have never Met me,” it said, almost sounding amused. “I have always been with you.”

I forced out the question. "Are you going to eat my eyes again?"

A moment of silence passed before the crow’s voice returned, this time lower, more ominous. "No," it said. "This time, it won’t be me."

The words hung heavy in the air, colder than the night itself, as if they carried a warning of something.

Grabbing the oil lamp from my bedside, I lit the flame and cautiously made my way to the door. The flickering light barely penetrated the thick shadows in the hallway. The usual dim lights that lined the corridor were off, and the space felt larger, almost as if the walls had expanded into some endless void.

I crouched down to inspect the liquid, and my suspicion was confirmed—it was gasoline. A thin, gleaming trail of it snaked down the hallway, leading somewhere deeper into the darkness. I took a brief second to consider, then made the decision to follow it. I needed to know where it led.

The corridor stretched impossibly long as I walked, my lamp casting eerie, dancing shadows on the walls. It felt as if I had been walking for hours, but when I glanced back, the room I had left was gone—swallowed by the blackness. There was no way back.

Panic clawed at my chest. I was trapped, lost in a nightmare that felt all too real. No matter how far I walked, the trail of gasoline continued, winding endlessly through the darkness beneath my feet. It reminded me of the dream with the streetlamps. The same suffocating darkness—but this time, there was no guiding lamplight to show the way.

Desperation overwhelmed me, and in a moment of irrationality, I struck a match and lit the gasoline. The flame sparked and quickly spread, illuminating the path ahead in an intense, orange glow.

For a moment, I felt a flicker of hope as the fire raced down the gasoline trail, lighting up the path that stretched ahead. The darkness receded just enough to reveal a destination—a wreck, suspended in time. Two cars, frozen in the moment of a collision, their front end crumpled, shards of glass hanging in mid-air. The scene was like something out of a twisted painting—smoke billowing but not moving, flames flickering but not consuming.

Inside one of the vehicles, I caught sight of the passengers—a family of four. Their faces were frozen in a mixture of fear and disbelief, eyes wide as they braced themselves for the impact. The mother clutched her child tightly to her chest, her arms wrapped around him in a desperate attempt to protect him from the inevitable collision. The scene felt suspended in time, their terror palpable in that split second before everything changed.

As I turned my attention to the other car, a strange sense of familiarity washed over me. Something about it tugged at my memory, an uneasy recognition creeping into my mind. I moved closer, hesitating with each step. My breath hitched in my throat as the realization hit me—it was unmistakable. That car wasn't just familiar; it was the very same make and model my father used to drive to work every day. Even the number plate was same, dented in a way I knew all too well, matched exactly. It was as if a ghost from my past had materialized in front of me, amplifying the eeriness of the moment.

Memories flooded back—my father's accident. The police calls , taunts of the neighbor's . The whispers of alcohol. The news of the crash had hit me like a sledgehammer when I was in college. I had never been to the scene of the accident, had never seen the wreckage with my own eyes. But now, it was as though I had been transported there.

I peered inside the car, expecting to see my father slumped over the wheel.

But it wasn't my father.

It was Raghav.

He sat motionless in the driver's seat, his face twisted in an expression of shock and agony, as if frozen in time. His body slumped awkwardly, yet there was something strange about him —he looked younger than I remembered, almost as if time had rewound itself. My mind raced with questions. How could this be Raghav? What was he doing here? How was any of this possible?

Before I could fully process what I was seeing, a strange rain began to fall. At first, I didn't even register the change, too stunned by the scene in front of me. But then I realized—it wasn't water that was cascading down from the sky. It was oil, thick and glistening, pouring down over the car and everything around it, but surprisingly not a single drop fell on me.

And then, without warning, the oil ignited. Flames erupted, consuming everything in their path with terrifying speed. The fire spread, devouring the car, the wreckage, and the ground beneath it. I stood there, frozen, helpless, unable to look away as the fire grew into an inferno. I could only watch as the flames swallowed the entire accident site. In what felt like an eternity, the fire finally died down, leaving behind nothing but smoldering ashes.

But as I stared at the charred remains, something caught my eye—a spark, flickering faintly within the ashes. I walked closer, squinting to make out what it was. There, nestled in the remnants of the wreckage, were two round objects, perfectly intact. As I approached, The hairs on my neck stood on end

They were eyeballs.

My stomach turned, and my mind rebelled against the sight. Yet somehow, deep down, I knew what I had to do. I hesitated, fear clawing at me, but something drove me forward. With trembling hands, I picked them up, my mind screaming at me to not do what i was about to do.

Without allowing myself time to think, I put the eyeballs into my mouth. I kept repeating to myself that this wasn't real, that I couldn't taste or feel anything. It was just a dream, after all.

But as soon as I swallowed them, A sharp, overwhelming darkness began to creep into my vision. My surroundings faded, and soon, I was plunged into total blackness. My own eyesight was gone, leaving me alone in a void which has now become altogether a familiar feeling.

CHAPTER 13

Collision Point

I can hear the faint sound of water pipes creaking in the walls filled the room. My thoughts came to me in disjointed fragments—an odd dream, a feeling of drowning in panic. But as my eyes focused, I realized something was wrong.

I wasn't in my bed.

The cold air smelled different, the sharp smell of something awful hung thick around me. I blinked rapidly, confused. I was standing in a bathroom, staring at a cracked mirror. The reflection staring back at me wasn't my own.

It was Raghav.

My heart nearly stopped as my brain scrambled to make sense of the image before me. I lifted a trembling hand, and Raghav's reflection followed suit, the movement eerily synchronized. This wasn't a dream. I wasn't myself anymore—I was seeing the world through Raghav's eyes .

I turned my head sharply, my vision blurring as I tried to orient myself. The cold tile beneath my feet felt real, the faint buzzing of the overhead light too sharp to be imagined. Maybe I am here to witness something.

Just then, the bathroom door creaked open. A casual voice cut through the silence.

"Hey, Raghav! You ready to go? Everyone's waiting."

I—Raghav—nodded automatically. I didn't control the motion, the body seemed to move on its own, responding as though I were merely a passenger inside it. I followed the other student out of the bathroom, my mind still spinning, trying to grasp the impossibility of the situation.

The hallway outside was bustling with life—students, groups of friends laughing and talking, their conversations a blurred background noise. The familiar smells of cheap cafeteria food and the faint trace of cigarette smoke lingered in the air. It was disorienting, almost surreal, watching everything unfold through Raghav's eyes. I soon realized this is the past

And then I saw him—me.

There I was, my younger self, carefree, walking with a group of friends, completely oblivious to the dark cloud that hung over me. Seeing myself that way, so innocent, so unaware of what was to come, made me pity myself. My—no, Raghav's—body tensed involuntarily, and before I could stop it, Raghav lunged toward younger me, hands outstretched as if to startle or scare him.

The younger version of me just stood there , brushing off Raghav's antics .

Suddenly, everything dissolved around me—the hallway, the students, the noise. The world shifted, like pages turning in a book. And then I was somewhere else entirely.

A dimly lit Dhaba. The flicker of yellow lights cast long shadows across the tables, and the sound of bottles clinking filled the small, cramped space. Raghav—drunk—was sitting at a table, slouched over with half-empty bottles scattered around him. I could feel the sluggishness in his movements, the dull buzz of intoxication clouding his mind. He laughed, but it was hollow, and his friends gradually faded into the shadows, leaving him alone.

Time stretched, the atmosphere thick with an odd sense of waiting. Raghav remained slouched at the table, his irritation building as if expecting something, or someone.

And then, a car pulled up outside, its headlights cutting through the dark. My stomach twisted painfully—I recognized the vehicle instantly.

I watched through Raghav's eyes as my father stepped out of the car and walked toward Raghav. He looked younger, tired lines etched across his face that were very familiar to me. Raghav looked up, his eyes glassy with alcohol, slurring his words.

"You're late," he muttered, struggling to stand.

"I'm sorry, sir," my father replied, his voice low and respectful. "Your father had me run some errands."

A suspicious frown crossed Raghav's face. "You didn't tell him where I was, did you?"

"No, sir," my father said quickly, his tone controlled, professional.

For a moment, Raghav's face softened, a smile creeping up his lips. He threw an arm around my father's shoulders in a sloppy gesture of camaraderie. "Good man, good man. Let's get outta here."

My father guiding him into the back seat. The ride started in an eerie silence, Raghav slouched against the window, eyes heavy from the alcohol.

"So, how are things at college ,sir?" , My father asked, trying to break the silence.

"why does that matter to you" , Raghav replied rudely.

"I just wanted to ask if you're getting along with my son?", My father inquired, with a concerned look on his face.

"Getting along? you think i hang out with that little bitch?" , Raghav replied with a mocking tone , " just do you job and drive"

My father went silent. After sometime Raghav's mood shifted, the silence replaced by an angry sharpness. Raghav leaned forward, tapping the back of my father's seat.

“Stop the car, I'll drive.”

My father tensed up. “Sir, you're drunk. It's not safe. you can't”

Raghav's anger flared suddenly. “What do you mean I can't drive? It's my-my father's car! I'll drive it whenever I damn well want!”

The car swerved slightly as Raghav grew louder, his temper sparking. I felt the rising tension through every nerve, my skin prickling with fear. His voice cut through the car like a knife. “You wanna lose your job?”

My father's hands tightened around the steering wheel, but he remained silent. His jaw clenched as he kept his eyes on the road, trying to keep his composure.

“Stop the car!” Raghav bellowed, kicking the back of the seat. “I said, stop the car!”

My father pulled over, his face drawn tight with suppressed frustration. Raghav stumbled out of the back seat, his body swaying as he forced his way into the driver's seat, shoving my father onto the gravel road.

I watched helplessly as my father stood on the side of the road, his face a mask of helpless anger as Raghav sped off into the night. The car lurched forward, accelerating down the dark, narrow road. Trees blurred by, the road ahead a tunnel of shadows.

Then, headlights appeared in the distance.

A car. Headed straight toward us.

I felt Raghav's panic as he swerved violently to avoid the

oncoming vehicle, but it was too late. The world tilted violently as the car spun out of control. I could feel Raghav's terror, his mind going blank as the vehicles collided with a deafening, silent crash.

And then everything stopped. Time itself froze.

I was pulled out of Raghav's body, I felt as if someone picked me up by pulling on the back of my shirt. i looked up , to see the bird picking me up with its beak, and then it placed me in on the ground

The scene before me was suspended in mid-motion—the crash, the wreckage, the shards of glass hanging like stars in the night.

"What is this?" I demanded, my voice trembling. "This can't be right. My father... he was the one who crashed. He went to jail for it. What am I seeing?"

The figure's voice was cold, mechanical. "This is the truth of that night"

A wave of dread washed over me. "How can this be, how can someone just hide a fact like this, was my father forced to take the blame for the accident?"

The figure remained silent, flickering like a dying flame. "No, this was not a conscious decision, even your father believes he was at fault."

I could barely breathe, my thoughts racing. "What about Raghav? Did he know? Did he hide this fact for all this time?"

"Raghav doesn't remember," the shadow whispered. "No one remembers except the ones responsible"

The truth struck me as a tidal wave. I thought back to the bruises on Raghav's face after the accident, the way he had returned to class, battered but silent. It all made sense now—pieces of the puzzle I had never put together. Raghav had been in the crash, but his memory of that night had been wiped away, leaving my father to take the blame.

The day after the crash, I was sitting at the breakfast table with my father, I noticed an unsettling silence between us. His expression was distant, almost vacant, as he stared blankly at his untouched plate. Concerned, I asked, "Dad, what's wrong? Why aren't you eating?"

He hesitated before replying, his voice heavy with sorrow. "I think I've done something terrible, son. I... I'll have to go away for a while."

"What do you mean? What did you do?", I asked.

I saw a deep sadness filling his eyes as he looked at me, his voice cracking. "I always dreamed of seeing you complete your studies, landing your first job... But I don't think I'll be around to see that." His words trailed off as tears welled up, spilling down his face. "Take care of your mother for me will you?"

Before I could process what he was saying, there was a loud knock at the door. A group of policemen entered, their uniforms imposing in the small room. Standing among them was a man with a white mustache, whom I immediately recognized. He looked at me and said "Haven't seen you in a while."

I was baffled. How could this man know me?

Without another word, the officers moved forward and handcuffed my father. I watched in stunned silence as they led him away. I followed them to the front door. Stepping outside, I saw our neighbors gathered, their faces a mixture of shock and curiosity, whispering among themselves as they watched the scene unfold.

With the realization of these memories, Anger surged inside me, raw and uncontrollable. My father is facing years in prison for a crime he didn't commit, while Raghav had lived his life as if nothing had happened. My hands shook with rage.

“There are forces at play here you do not understand,” the bird said softly, its voice cutting through the chaos in my mind.

I stared at the figure before me, My lungs seized up. "Who are you? Why are you helping me recover these memories?" I asked, my voice barely above a whisper, filled with confusion and desperation.

The figure's form flickered, becoming sharper, more distinct, until it seemed almost human—but not quite. "I am you," it said softly, "or at least, a piece of you."

"I don’t understand," I replied, shaking my head, my thoughts swirling in a chaotic fog.

"I, too, was taken from you," it explained, "just like these memories. But I found my own place, made a nest elsewhere."

"Why?" I asked, feeling the weight of the question, tears threatening to spill. "Why am I forgetting things that are so important to me? Please, tell me!"

"You will learn that, just as you did once before. All you need to do is listen."

With that, the creature extended its beak—a sleek, dark thing—dropping a small, familiar pouch into my trembling hand.

I stared at the pouch, feeling its strange weight, a heaviness that wasn’t just physical. When I looked back up, the bird was gone, disappearing as quietly as it had come. Once again, I was left alone. Alone at the crash site. The isolation was stifling, and a sense of dread pressed down on me. I had no idea how to get back to my room. The crow had vanished without leaving a single clue, as if my path forward was something I had to unravel on my own.

I looked down at the pouch. Hesitating for only a moment, I gently opened it, only to see an endless void within the small bag. Cautiously, I slid my hand inside, expecting to feel the bottom, but instead, my arm sank deeper, far more than the bag's size should allow. It seemed endless, a strange abyss within.

I kept searching, my fingers brushing through the darkness, hoping to find something that would make sense of all this. Eventually, I felt it—a small, round object with an unusual texture. I grabbed it, curiosity and dread warring inside me. As I pulled it out, a sharp, agonizing pain shot through me.

I screamed, dropping to my knees, my hand instinctively reaching for my face. To my horror, one of my eyes was gone. My face felt blank, empty where my eye had once been. Panic set in, but at the same time, a disturbing clarity began to dawn on me.

I understood then. Just like before—like when I consumed the eyes of Raghav and saw fragments of his memories—this was the price. If I wanted to recover my own memories, I would have to eat my own eyes.

Gripped by a morbid determination, I thrust my hand back into the pouch, searching for the other eye. I found it quickly, the cold sphere resting against my fingertips. Pulling it out, I felt my vision blur until it vanished completely. I was plunged into total darkness, blind.

But there was no turning back. I knew what I had to do.

Without hesitating further, I brought the eyes to my mouth and consumed them, one by one.

CHAPTER 14

Deja Vu

I woke up slowly, my mind clouded with the kind of heavy, disorienting fog that settles in after being unconscious for too long. Sleep hadn't felt like rest; it had been more like drifting through a haze of fragmented dreams, none of which I could fully remember. I blinked sluggishly, trying to shake the weight from my eyelids, but the world around me remained unfocused and distant.

For a moment, I couldn't remember where I was. Everything felt disjointed. Then it hit me—I was in my hostel room, my own bed. The faint scent of dampness and old textbooks hung in the air, unmistakable. My senses returned slowly .

A dull, throbbing ache pulsed through my right leg, a warning that something had gone horribly wrong. I tried to sit up, but as soon as I moved, an excruciating, sharp pain shot through my leg, freezing me in place. My breath hitched, and a soft hiss escaped my lips as I clutched the bed. Panic surged through me, more intense than the pain itself.

On the wooden table next to my bed, something caught my eye. Squinting through the dim light, I could make out the shapes of the cricket ball and a folded piece of paper, both resting atop the table. it was the letter that drew my attention now. My name was scribbled on the front in hurried handwriting, and I instantly recognized it as Arjun's.

I stared at the note for a moment, a strange feeling of déjà vu creeping over me. Slowly, I reached out, my fingers trembling as I grabbed the letter and unfolded it. The spidery, slanted handwriting was unmistakable—it was Arjun's.

But that's when it hit me.

The fall. The letter. The bandages. I feel a sense of Deja vu. The same exact sequence of events had already played out once before. My breath quickened as I struggled to understand what was happening. This wasn't just familiar .

I turned the letter over, expecting the strange scribbles I had seen the last time: "The pouch, the ball, fire, Father, streetlights." But the back of the letter was blank. No strange markings. Nothing like what i remembered.

My heart pounded louder in my ears as confusion took over. How could I be reliving the same moment? My mind raced, flashing back to the shadowy figure that had appeared before, the one that had given me the pouch. The pouch. Where was it?

I looked down at my hands, hoping to find the pouch clutched tightly in my fist like before. But my hands were empty.

"What's going on?" I muttered under my breath, trying to make sense of the unravelling reality. There was something wrong, something off about this entire situation, but I couldn't put my finger on it. The memory of this moment felt incomplete, like a dream slipping through my grasp the harder I tried to hold on to it.

It was already 3 pm when I woke up, I had a throbbing pain and a massive headache, I decided to eat the food Arjun had left me, and I decided to lay on the bed and get some rest.

* * *

Hours passed. The sun slowly disappeared beneath the horizon, plunging the room into shadow. I haven't moved from my bed. My mind was too tangled, too consumed by the overwhelming sensation that time itself had twisted. I could feel it—this wasn't the reality I had left behind.

As the room grew darker, the familiar weight of sleep began to pull at me, but I fought it. I didn't trust what might happen if I allowed myself to slip into unconsciousness again that night. Not after the strange events that kept replaying in my mind.

Tonight was a full moon. The kind of night where the sky seems almost too vast, too silent, the moon hanging there like an ancient eye watching over everything. As I sat in my room, the soft, silver light of the moon filtered through the window, brushing the floor and walls with its pale, ethereal glow. There was a stillness in the air, a strange sense of calm that stood in stark contrast to the chaos happening inside my mind — the noise, the endless spinning of life beyond these four walls. For a moment a feeling washed over me, as though time itself had slowed, like the night held its breath.

My gaze drifted to the mirror on the far wall. It caught the moon's reflection, perfect and round, framed by the faint glow of moonlight. It was as if another world existed in that reflection — the moon, unburdened by clouds or shadows, resting in the glass like a secret only I was allowed to witness. I found myself staring at it, losing track of time, the minutes slipping away as my thoughts grew distant and dreamlike.

And then The moon blinked.

I wasn't sure at first. My tired eyes must have been playing tricks on me. But there it was, undeniable: the top and bottom edges of the moon drew together like eyelids, closing slowly, deliberately, before parting again. I sat frozen, disbelieving, trying to process what I was seeing. The moon blinked again, slower this time, as if it were growing more confident, more aware of my gaze. It blinked once, twice more, and then stopped — as though satisfied that it had been noticed.Then pupils began to form on it. it began to look like a proper eye, then suddenly. It moved its pupils, subtly, like a snake testing the air for vibrations. At first, I thought I imagined it, but then it happened again—those dark pupils, glossy and vacant, seemed to be drawn toward the corner of the room. A sliver of movement so slight, it barely disrupted the stillness.

Compelled by some dark instinct, I followed its gaze, my eyes drifting reluctantly to the shadowy corner. And in that moment, my heart sank into a pit of cold dread. The nightmare I thought I had shaken off—the one I had convinced myself was just a product of my fevered mind—was back. Not merely in memory, but here, manifest, more real than the very air I was breathing.

There it was again, the shape. A figure, hunched, almost crumpled. Its white back was turned to me, yet I knew without needing to see its face—that it was the same horrific presence I had seen before the fall. The same grotesque thing that had haunted my peripheral vision during my wake. But this time, something was different.

This time, I wasn't paralyzed. I could move.

The awareness washed over me like a splash of ice water. My breath was erratic, short, almost strangled gasps, but I was in control of my limbs. Not helpless like before. A flicker of defiance stirred inside me—whether it was fear, anger, or sheer frustration, I wasn't sure, but I grabbed the first thing I could find, the ball resting on the bedside table. My fingers curled around its surface, slick with sweat.

I hurled it at the figure, half-expecting—no, hoping—to feel the sick thud of contact. Instead, the ball sailed through it as if through mist, vanishing into the corner without a sound. For a moment, I was too stunned to react. My pulse stilled.

The figure cast no shadow.

That's when the truth hit me—it wasn't real. Or at least, not real in the way physical things are real. This was something else, an illusion, a trick of some kind, or perhaps something more sinister. Something trying to manipulate me, to drag me back into the abyss of fear.

But I wouldn't go so easily this time.

I fumbled for the light switch next to the bed, my fingers brushing against the cold metal. With a sharp click, the room was flooded with a harsh, artificial glow. The figure, the haunting presence, dissolved almost immediately, evaporating into the air as if made of smoke and shadows. But even as it disappeared, something else moved at the edge of my vision—a quick, skittering movement.

There, in the dim light, I saw it. A small, grotesque creature, barely visible, its elongated limbs clawing frantically at the floor as it scurried toward the corner, as if in retreat. It was running away towards the shadows.

Ignoring the sharp, stabbing pain in my leg, I pushed myself out of bed, wincing as the weight of my body pressed against my injury. I reached for the crutch propped nearby and limped toward the corner, my heart hammering in my chest. Adrenaline coursed through my veins, dulling the ache. I shoved aside a stack of old boxes, half-forgotten relics piled against the wall, clearing the space where the creature had vanished.

And there, hidden beneath layers of dust and discarded papers, was the pouch.

I stared at it for a long moment, my mind reeling with a thousand possibilities. Why here? Why now? My hands trembled as I picked it up, the worn texture rough beneath my fingertips. The pouch felt heavier than it should have, as though it carried more than just the weight of its contents. Something shifted inside as I turned it over in my hands.

Slowly, carefully, I limped back to the bed, needing the support as I sat down, feeling the pressure of the moment settle over me like a dark cloud. With deliberate movements, I opened the pouch. Inside, there was a small, tightly wrapped object—a note, bound with a thin piece of string. A knot twisted in my stomach as I untied it, the string unravelling in my fingers.

It wasn't a note. It was a palm-leaf manuscript, ancient and brittle, covered in strange symbols. The surface was worn, time-stained, with lines and markings that spiraled in ways I couldn't comprehend. I traced the symbols with my fingers, the rough texture of the leaf sending shivers up my spine. What did these markings mean? Were they some long-lost language? Or a code meant for me alone?

Then, without warning, a low, guttural sound broke the silence.

I froze. The noise came from the corner—the same corner where the creature had fled. It was a voice, deep and distorted, muttering in a language I didn't recognize. My skin prickled, but then something even stranger happened.

The markings on the palm leaf began to shift, rearranging themselves right before my eyes. The symbols twisted and coiled, reforming into words—words I couldn't fully understand but somehow, on a deeper level, understand.

Give it back.

CHAPTER 15

Beneath the Lies

I gazed down at the leaf in my trembling hands as the guttural sounds from the corner of the room grew louder. The strange symbols on the palm leaf, which seemed meaningless, began to shift and reshape before my eyes, revealing their meaning. Though I had never seen such markings before, they spoke directly to my mind, as if unlocking something hidden within me.

The words on the leaf matched the creature's voice: "I know you, child of forgotten past."

My body shook as I glanced towards the shadowy corner. The deep, ancient voice continued its chant, but now I understood it, as though the leaf had opened a door in my mind.

"What are you?" I asked, my voice trembling, but just clear enough to break through the murmurs.

The shape shifted slightly and responded more clearly, each word creeping through the air: "**Moi Bira**."

Bira?I have heard that name before.I remember Grandma mentioning them in one of her tales. She use to tell me stories about these nasty little Creatures. They were malevolent spirits capable of possessing and tormenting people. In these stories they are unleashed upon a family by someone wishing to bring them harm.

"So .. you things are real? "

"As real as you are", the voice replied.

But what do you want from me.. did someone send you here to harm me?" I asked.

"No, there is no need for me to harm you" the creature replied.

"Why scare me with your illusions then?Was that really necessary?" I questioned.

"I needed to give you nightmares, so that I could feed on them."

My heart pounded as I stared at the hidden form, barely visible. "You... feed on nightmares? as in dreams?"

"Yes," the Bira replied, its voice softening, almost as if pleading. "It is how I survive, how I exist in this world. It is necessary."

I fell silent, disbelief washing over me. "You said you know me? How?"

"I remember your face, someone familiar. Someone whose memories I've touched before," the voice whispered.

"What do you mean? you've messed with my memories before? But why?" I pressed.

"I was asked to."

Confusion clouded my thoughts as the Bira began explaining, It started to tell me everything about the fragmented memories of my father , the accident, and the inconsistencies in his trial and everything else i had forgotten. Suddenly, like a stack of dominos falling one by one the gaps in my memories began to fill. I began to remember the whole truth.

"You... you erased my memories. You made everyone forget the truth about my father."

The Bira shifted again, its voice growing quieter. "I did what I was asked to, for a price."

"Who? who asked you to do that?" I demanded.

"A man with a large moustache."

As i realised who it was, Anger surged through me as I clenched the manuscript tightly, blood rushing in my ears. "Raghav's father? It was him wasn't it? He erased everything, from everyones mind but his. He made my father rot in jail? made him bear guilt that wasn't his while the real culprit walks free every day?"

The creature sensed my fury.

"What price did he pay for all this?" I asked.

"His son."

"Raghav? But he's doing fine isn't he? He has lived guilt-free all these years."

"Whatever Dreams Raghav had, they were all sacrificed on his father's whim. more than once even. "

Then it dawned on me what the Bira meant. I started thinking back to our early years, when Raghav had been so ambitious and full of hope for the future. Every time he spoke of his desire of being a great cricketer his eyes would light up. I recalled how promising and full of hope he was. When he played at the district level once Nothing seemed to be able to stop him back then. Everyone thought he was bound for greatness because of his indisputable talent. However, as the years went by, something changed. Raghav's enthusiasm for cricket diminished. He stopped playing, stopped mentioning the dreams that had once defined him. At the time, I had assumed that like so many others, he had simply given up—perhaps life had worn him down, or maybe he'd chosen a different path. I hadn't thought much of it beyond that.

Now, though, with the Bira's revelation, the truth became painfully clear. It wasn't that Raghav had given up; he had forgotten entirely. His dreams had been stolen from him, erased like they had never existed. I could picture him as a boy, filled with hopes that would one day be stripped away, leaving only a hollow shell of the person he was meant to be.

I felt sympathy for him for the first time. Without his knowledge, his life had changed.

However, despite this outpouring of empathy, it was unable to take away my personal pain or the resentment that still clung to me.

Raghav's still lived a considerably good life, But the injustice that my father faced was the price. I was at my breaking point, I could not hold myself back any longer, "I want to make them pay. They have destroyed everything i loved to protect themselves, they set up my father. And who knows how many heinous acts they have concealed from the public?"

I caught a sight of the Bira's shape for the first time as it moved, its long legs clinging to the wall like a spider. "Yes, revenge". With eagerness, it responded, "I can give you that.I can make them forget something important, something that will lead to their ruin."

Emotion overwhelmed me, and anger boiled inside. "Do it," I said, my voice raw with rage. "Make them suffer."

"There is always a price", it warned.

"what is it? " i asked.

"Your anger, your hate. I will take it from you, and you will not remember what you've done, Are you ready to give that up?", The Bira explained.

NO, not that. I need to remember .If i force them to pay for their crimes, i need to stay and collect the debt.

"This deal, what do you have in it for you? surely it benifits you somehow?", I asked.

The Bira kept silent for some time, than it began explaining , "I feed on meat because I am able to.I feast on dreams because i am required to. But the deeper emotions inside your heart like hate ,love, Aspirations they are what i Want to eat. do you understand?"

I understood now, why it explained everything to me. It showed me the truth so that i would feel this rage.So that it can benifit from it.I assume it needs some kind of permission in the form of a deal to feed on more complex feelings.

I gave it some more thaught. I could not decide what I wanted more. To destroy them or to remember their destruction. I tried to concentrate all my rage to take a decision , then a plan begin to form.

I decided to bet everything on it.

"Do it", I said without hesitation.

I could feel a smile forming on the Bira's face. "Very well", it said. And without a moments notice begant to sprint towards me. I was too late to react as it grabbed on to my face. It did what it had to do and than disappeared into the shadows of my room once again.

Panic surged through me as the world spun. Desperate, I grabbed a pen and the note Arjun had left me. I needed to write something down , anything .With trembling hands, I scribbled down what I could—the pouch, the ball, the Bira, the accident. I could not concentrate enough to write more than few words. I put the leaf inside the pouch and dropped it on top of the paper.

But the dizziness intensified, my vision darkened, and as soon as I got on my bed I went to a deep slumber.

* * *

My surroundings come into focus. I was in my bed, sunlight spilling through the window. The pain in my leg was still there, dull but constant.

Arjun was sitting beside me, a concerned look on his face. "Good morning," he said softly. "You've been asleep for a while."

I rubbed my eyes, "How long was I asleep?"

"It's almost noon" Arjun replied, handing me a glass of water. "Listen, I have some news. I wasn't sure when to tell you, but... Raghav's family... their house burned down last night."

I froze, the glass halfway to my lips. "What?"

"They're saying someone left the gas on, and it caused an explosion. His entire family was inside," Arjun said, his voice quiet and sombre.

A strange, cold sensation crept through my body. His heart beat erratically, but my mind couldn't grasp the emotion. I found myself smiling—a strange, hollow smile .

"hey, when I fell through the window, how many days was I out for?" I asked

"You were asleep for whole Two days , even though the doctor said you'd wake up in a day"

"Two days?" I thought, confused. Last month was February. I fell on the 28th and woke up on the first—shouldn't that have been just one day?

But right than I realised, "Arjun... this year is a leap year, right?" I asked.

"Yeah, why?" he replied.

"Oh.. I get it now". Without realizing it, I began to laugh, a low chuckle that quickly grew into something darker. I held my hands in front of my face, staring at them as if they belonged to someone else. My laughter echoed through the room, sharp and unsettling.

Arjun stared at me, his eyes wide with confusion and fear. "Ishan... what's wrong with you?"

But I didn't answer. I only laughed, with a manic, almost delirious sound .

* * *

It has been around ten months since the fire that destroyed Raghav's home. The charred remains of the once-proud mansion stood motionless and empty, a skeleton of ash and soot against the dull afternoon sky. The lingering stench of burning wood and devastation filled the air, a sobering reminder of the atrocity that had occurred here.

Standing beside the ruins of the house, I could still feel the tiny tinge of old agony in my bones, even though my leg was fully healed. I looked at the pieces of what had been, the charred remains, the broken foundation. The wind rustling through the trees around them sounded hollow, like if the world had gone still.

My breathe formed a small cloud in the cool air. I began to speak.

"I guess I won the bet", I said with a sign of relief on my face .

The day i met the Bira I realised something. When It steals the memories of people, the effect is not permanant. There is a way to cheat past it. If someone it effects is confronted with enough evidence of Alteration ,the truth begin to crumble, and with enough of a push the memories come back. I figured it out when the Bira revealed to me the truths about my father.

That day when i made the deal with it i was planning to write everything down so that i could recall it again.But i guess you saw through it and reacted as soon as I agreed to the deal. I could only write down hints to the truth with the time i had but it was not enough. I was about to lose everything. But that's where the bird comes in.

"That Bird... I understand now what it was . All the distrust and hate I had harbored for so many years, as well as the rage I experienced on realizing the truth.I think it was too fundamental and profound to simply vanish.All those strong emotions, they found a way to settle within the deepest parts of my mind. And when the time came, it provided me the push i needed, it made sure I enjoyed seeing things through to the end. What good would Vengence be if no one remembered, it would becomes an empty gesture."

Behind me, standing in the shadow of a narrow alleyway that stretched between two charred walls, the Bira waited. Its dark, shifting form was nearly invisible in the gloom, but I could feel its presence . The creature has always been with me since that night, lurking just outside the reach of light, tethered to me by the choices that we made together.

I turned slightly, my eyes glancing back toward the alley, though I didn't need to see the Bira to know it was there.

"It seems you can't stray too far from this pouch " I said, my tone almost casual as I reached into my pocket, feeling the touch of the familiar object. The pouch that held the Bira at bay. "So I'll keep you near me."

"I tire of eating meat," the Bira whispered. "I hunger for more."

My lips curled into a faint, grim smile. I wasn't afraid of the creature anymore. I knew what it was, what it needed. And for now, I had control. The Bira could twist reality, but it couldn't act without direction, and it couldn't harm anyone physically. I made sure it was bound to me, just as I was bound to it.

"I guess you'll have to stay hungry for now," I replied, unflinching. "Until I say otherwise."

I didn't look back as I walked away, my thoughts already moving forward, beyond the ashes, beyond the ruins of my old life. There was no more confusion, no more doubt. I understood now. The shadow that had once haunted me was a part of me now, as much as my own anger and resentment had been. And though the Bira's hunger still lingered, waiting for the day it would be fed again, I was in control.

I walked toward the horizon, the burnt house shrinking in the distance. I had made my choice, and now there was no turning back.

The past had been buried, the future was mine to shape, and the shadows were no longer something to fear.

They were mine to command.

ABOUT THE AUTHOR

Kaushik Baruah

I love a good story in any form it takes - whether through movies, TV series, books, comics, manga, anime, or video games. When I'm not navigating the demands of work life, I spend my time exploring these different ways stories can be told.

This is my first book, and I wrote it with the hope to create a story that works not just on paper, but could someday come alive as an interactive experience. My hope is to eventually take my characters and their world from the written page into a video game that you can play through yourself.

I hope you enjoyed being part of this story.

Email me at : blackwingbtw@gmail.com

www.ingramcontent.com/pod-product-compliance
Lightning Source LLC
LaVergne TN
LVHW012112160826
845678LV00014B/3054
* 9 7 8 9 3 3 4 1 7 5 2 7 1 *